For ɟy ...

No Missing Parts

And Other Stories about Real Princesses

Anne Laurel Carter

No Missing Parts
And Other Stories about Real Princesses

Anne Laurel Carter

Red Deer Press

The Publisher
Red Deer Press
813 MacKimmie Library Tower
2500 University Drive NW
Calgary Alberta Canada
T2N 1N4
www.reddeerpress.com

Credits
Cover design by Duncan Campbell
Cover image courtesy of Wayne Eardly/Masterfile
Text design by Dennis Johnson
Printed and bound in Canada by Friesens for Red Deer Press

Acknowledgments
"The Piano Lesson" originally appeared in *Up All Night,* edited by R.T. MacIntyre, Thistledown Press, 2001. It appears courtesy of Thistledown Press. Financial support provided by the Canada Council, the Department of Canadian Heritage and the Alberta Foundation for the Arts, a beneficiary of the Lottery Fund of the Government of Alberta, and the University of Calgary.

THE CANADA COUNCIL | LE CONSEIL DES ARTS
FOR THE ARTS | DU CANADA
SINCE 1957 | DEPUIS 1957

National Library of Canada Cataloguing in Publication Data
Carter, Anne, 1953–
No missing parts
ISBN 0-88995-253-1
1. Title.
PS8555.A7727N62 2002   jC813'.54   C2002-910434-3
PZ7.C2427NO 2002

5 4 3 2 1

To Peter Carver
for his love of story

Contents

No Missing Parts

And Other Stories about Real Princesses

A Note from the Author

I HAVE A SOFT SPOT for a good love story. It doesn't matter whether it's set now or five hundred years ago. The main character doesn't have to be rich or beautiful. In fact, I prefer a story about a more ordinary girl—someone struggling to find her identity, someone who has to think her way through life's problems.

A small misfortune in my life is that I was raised mostly on fairy tales such as *Sleeping Beauty* and *Cinderella*. The adult in me knows Snow White looks ridiculous asleep in her casket waiting for a kiss. The little girl I was did not.

Every so often I find the notion of being saved still lurking in the deepest corner of my adult mind. How I wish I'd been raised on stories of other princesses—independent young women who, throughout the ages, took leadership, defied social conformity, and were smart enough to banish evil from their home, whatever its guise. It has taken me years to appreciate that love, in all its many forms, saves us, but never appears as a handsome prince. The challenge is one of looking deeper, beneath an exterior. Love has many guises, too, and may arrive looking like a frog . . . which will remain a frog.

I see now that I wrote these stories for the girl inside of me. But also for the many beautiful women who have blessed my life: my mother, my sister, my daughter, my friends.

What a grand adventure to be a girl.

The Legend of
Princess Sheila NaGeira

ONCE MANY CENTURIES AGO, in the west of Ireland, there lived a lonely queen who wanted more than anything to have children. But she was frail and poor in health, and it was only with the help of three crones that she was finally able to conceive and carry a child to full term. Her labor was long and painful, and the king and his court waited impatiently for news of the birth.

At last the queen's handmaid opened the doors to the queen's chamber and spoke. "The queen has given birth to a girl. You may enter," she said, beginning to weep, "and pay your last respects to the queen."

Inside the chamber, the queen lay upon her bed, cradling the infant princess in her arms. Bearing a child had taken all her strength, and the pallor of death covered her in its cold, white sheet.

"Call the crones," the queen whispered to her husband, "that they might grant me my death wish."

The king's face twisted sharply with fear, then anger. He was a man accustomed to dominating others. Were these crones not fairies who drew their powers from another world? Why should the queen burden him, the living, with the results of such a risky request? Yet his queen was loved and respected, and before his court, pride cautioned the king to stall. Pretending concern for his wife, the king consulted his advisors—men who loved the sound of their own voices. They would argue for as long as it took the queen to conveniently die.

While they debated, the queen's fastest pigeon flew unnoticed from the open window, carrying the queen's request. Before the candle at the queen's side could finish its burning, the crones arrived in her chamber, much to the king's dismay.

The fairy women gathered around the queen's bed. Their long, white hair rose and twined like branches of a wintry forest above her still body. Within the stone walls of the great chamber, the air filled with the smells of another world.

The queen opened her eyes, and the eldest crone smiled sadly. "Dear queen, you have the child of your longing. Now you ask us to grant your death wish, knowing that a death wish can never be undone."

Tenderly, the queen caressed the silky skin of her baby's cheek. "Thank-you for your help. I'm only sorry that I shall not live to see my daughter grow into a woman. Show me her future, so that I may know what lies ahead for her and choose my wish wisely."

The three crones gazed at one another, then at the baby. Their eyes glowed brightly as they began to pierce the mystery of the infant's future.

Shielding their eyes from the intense light over the queen's bed, the king and his court trembled as the eldest crone spoke in an ancient voice. "You will name your daughter Sheila NaGeira. Though she will always be a princess, she will never make her home in a king's castle. She will be a princess of the forest, strong and wild as the trees and creatures who make it their home."

The king's shocked cry echoed throughout the palace. What kind of a princess would reject her father's magnificent world?

But the queen smiled with contentment and nodded for the crones to continue.

The second fairy spoke. "Born of the rocky island, your daughter shall be a daughter of the sea, full of storm and fierce in battle. No man shall rule her."

The whole court gasped with disapproval. The king turned to consult his chief advisor. A virtuous woman had meek and submissive ways, obeying her husband with a sweet countenance. Surely he could command a wish on behalf of the delirious queen before it was too late?

But before he could interfere, the queen nodded again for the crones to continue. Here on her deathbed, she saw all too clearly the folly of submission and weakness.

The third crone spoke. "The princess shall have grace and beauty. Men shall look upon your daughter with desire. Yet when she looks at them, none will be equal to the strength of her gaze. All will look away, unworthy."

This time, the queen herself cried out. This last prophecy filled her heart with anguish. She did not want her daughter's life to be dominated by loneliness.

"I do not wish a loveless fate for my daughter," she said. "Grant me my death wish: let my daughter find a worthy man to love."

The crones consulted amongst themselves. They could no more change the princess's nature and destiny than they could change the rise and fall of the tides. But they were fond of the queen, moved to pity, and bound to grant her death wish.

After a lengthy consultation, the third crone spoke again. "We have found a way to grant your wish, O Queen. The princess must find a man who loves the forest and sea with a fierceness to match her own. He must choose freedom over riches. If he would prove himself worthy of her love, he too must forsake a king's inheritance. But she cannot influence his choice in any way if she is to believe him a prince among men."

No sooner were these words uttered than the king turned his back on his wife and daughter, and stormed from the queen's chamber. What perversity! He would find a way to thwart these women and crush this willful daughter.

But the queen smiled graciously and thanked the crones. A humble hut—if filled with love—was a far happier fate than a cold, heartless castle. She gave the infant princess one final kiss before she closed her eyes, at peace at last.

IN THE MONTHS FOLLOWING the queen's death, the princess's tiny presence in the castle weighed heavily upon the king. He married again and was eager to remove the threat of this unwanted issue of his line.

Fearing the crones' wrath, he knew he could not have the princess killed. So instead he called the crones and slyly suggested that they raise the girl on a distant rugged coast as they pleased. The crones saw through his selfish motives but laughed silently. Why inform the king that this was the perfect way to fulfill Sheila NaGeira's destiny?

They agreed but insisted upon one condition: "When the

princess is seventeen, she will return to be presented with suitors and her inheritance. If a suitor is able to win her heart, you must accept her choice and obey her command."

And so the years passed. Raised on the rugged coast by the crones, far from the company of men, Sheila became everything the crones had foreseen: a princess of the forest and sea, with a temperament to match the wind. Riding her horse on a hunt, her black hair flowed behind her like wings of the night. The crones delighted in teaching her any and all manner of craft and skill. As a result Sheila grew strong and independent, as skilled with sword and arrow as she was with herbs and words of comfort.

Much to the king's dismay, it was not tales of Sheila's character that spread across the land. Rather, reports of her beauty began to spread far and wide. As her seventeenth birthday approached, the king's court began to fill with wealthy, handsome suitors, each hoping to claim Princess Sheila NaGeira for his wife.

The evening before her seventeenth birthday, Sheila bade a reluctant farewell to the crones. The forests overlooking the ocean cliffs were her home. She had known only happiness here. But the crones were insistent. They recounted word for word the events of her birth and her mother's death wish.

"Your mother left you a precious gift. Of all people, she knew what it meant to live in the absence of love. Somewhere there lives a man worthy of your love. The time has come for you to find him."

Sheila's eyes flashed as she mounted her horse. "There is no such man alive. Why should I leave? You have loved me as daughter and sister and friend. Why must I change?"

The crones hid their grief behind a wall of stony faces.

"Have we taught you nothing? A tree grows tall in the forest only to fall in a storm and scatter its seeds. The tide pounds the face of the hardest cliff and softens it over time. Nothing and no one can hide from the laws of the world. You were always meant to leave us. Ride now. Return to your father. Look honestly into your suitors' eyes as we have taught you, and do not look away if you find a prince among men."

Black hair fighting the wind, tears spilling faster than her horse's hooves, Sheila flew from her childhood like a storm cloud. She rode all night toward her father's palace. With the dawn, her fury finally spent, she arrived and was led by a servant to her father's court. In her sturdy, leather boots, Sheila walked the stony corridors that had been her mother's home. She was about to meet her father and her suitors. Her future beckoned. Her spirits rose to answer the call of adventure.

In the Great Hall, she was ordered to kneel before an older, black-haired man seated on a throne.

"Daughter," he said in a cold, imperious tone. "Rise so we may examine you."

Sheila stood. She stared at the king. He stared at her. The shape of his face was surprisingly like her own, but strangely, not its expression. An arrogant contempt glittered in his green eyes. Sheila was immediately on her guard.

In seventeen years of living with the crones and the villagers who came seeking help, she had never felt a gaze like her father's: it wanted to crush her very essence. She suddenly imagined her mother's unhappy life and was filled with pity.

Curious, still hopeful, Sheila gazed at the rest of her father's court. In one face after another, she met scorn and rejection. Standing amidst the silk and fancy brocade, with her hair wild and loose over her simple gown, Sheila felt a loneliness she had never before experienced.

Behind her father stood the suitors in silk and velvet. She studied them carefully and longed to return to the high hills overlooking the sea. Not a man in the room pleased her eye or her spirit.

One by one, the suitors were introduced. She met them with an honest gaze, as the crones had taught her. They gaped at the beauty in her face and figure, and she reflected back to them all that was in their own hearts: lust, greed, disdain, conquest, and the desire to dominate. One by one, each suitor was forced to shield his eyes and turn away, unable to stand their own reflections.

The court soon emptied. The king stared at Sheila. "Daughter," he sneered, "look what you've done! You have been cursed since birth to be a willful, unlovable woman. No man will ever love you. Answer carefully, Sheila. Was there none here today you would agree to marry?"

Cursed? What could her father mean? His words tore into her heart, stirring up doubt. Just then, the shutter on the window blew open and a great wind tore through the room. The words of the crones' prophecies echoed off the great stone walls: *she is a princess of the forest and the sea*. The court was not meant to be her home.

No man will rule her. She'd looked honestly for a prince amongst these men. He was not here.

She held her head high. "No, sire. There was none here that pleased me."

A wicked delight burned in the king's eyes. "If none in this court is good enough for you, I will send you to your aunt's convent in France, where you may live out your days in obedience, if not to men . . . then to God."

Sheila's bright green eyes flashed back in defiance. "I far prefer the convent to anything I have seen here today."

"Then away with you. Away," he ordered, calling his men. "Take her with this chest of gold to Captain Donahue's ship. It leaves tonight for France. Her destiny will be to live her days in a convent, shut away from this world and all men."

At dawn the next morning, Captain Donahue ordered the ship to set sail. Standing on deck, Sheila watched her homeland disappear on the dark horizon. The rugged shoulders of the coast seemed to heave sadly as the ship rocked upon the sea. Everything the crones had foretold was happening. She would not live in a king's court. No man ruled her.

Nevertheless, she was filled with loneliness at the prospect of exile, banished from her homeland, with only a heavy chest of gold as her inheritance.

Her father's last words haunted her. *Away with you, away.*

TWO DAYS LATER, Sheila woke to the sharp crack of cannon fire. Growing up, she'd heard many stories about the nations of Europe fighting their battles on the English Channel. Sheila took her sword and climbed on deck to enter the melee of shouting and swords ringing in battle. A ship loomed beside theirs. Its men were swarming over the gunwales. A fierce battle raged across the deck; Irish crewmen fell wounded and bloody before her eyes.

Baffled, Sheila looked up to see England's flag upon the invader's ship and the queen's uniform upon its men. Why would an English ship attack them? And then, right before her eyes, a young red-coated officer of the Queen's Navy chased, then held at sword point, her own Captain Donahue.

Her own sword in hand, Sheila leapt to his defense.

Captain Donahue turned his head toward her, but the English officer turned too, just in time to face Sheila. A lively, handsome face caught Sheila off guard for the half-second needed to sidestep her advance. Sheila lunged into thin air and the attacker flicked her sword from her hand.

"A fearless maiden on the high seas who defends her captain! What an honor. I am Lieutenant Gilbert Pike, at your service," the handsome officer said with a gallant bow.

Trapped at the end of his sword beside Captain Donahue, Sheila tried to gain the upper hand. "By all appearances you would be in service to Elizabeth, Queen of England. By whose order do you attack a ship of her ally, my father, the King of Ireland?"

For a brief second, Sheila thought she saw regret flicker across Lieutenant Gilbert Pike's face.

"You're right, my lady. We do wear the queen's uniform, but for our own purposes. We are no longer her servants. We attack as free men under the orders of Captain Easton."

"That would be me you're speaking of, would it not, Lieutenant Pike?" roared a voice behind them.

Sheila turned to find an immense, gray-haired man staring at them. He wore a black, plumed hat and had a round drinker's belly that spoke of self-indulgence.

"It would, sir. Here is the captain of the Irish vessel and his passenger, an Irish princess."

Captain Easton lifted a jug in mock salute to Sheila, then held it to his lips. The clear liquid poured into his mouth and spilled down the front of his jacket. After a long swig, he wiped his lips and belched with satisfaction.

"Peter Easton, at your command," he roared again, drunk with the success of his battle and its spoils. He stared at the remnants of the Irish crew, now huddled in defeat before him. "I'm your new captain, if you choose to sail with me. Those of you who do not," he laughed, "why, you're welcome to remain on board your own ship." He made a mocking bow to Sheila. "And how fortunate to make the acquaintance of a princess and"—he pointed to the chest of gold—"her inheritance. Lieutenant, how much would you wager this girl's safe return means to her father?"

Sheila interrupted coldly. "My father sends me to a convent in France. You'll get no ransom for me. I'll stay with his ship."

"A willful girl, I see. And probably in the way of most girls sent to a convent. No wonder your father would be rid of you. By all means," he sneered, "stay on the ship."

Boldly, Gilbert Pike raised his sword in the air. "I say we bring the maiden with us. Who knows? Her father may have a change of heart one day and pay a rich ransom."

The captain stared warily at his lieutenant, then said, "It's hard to find an officer as brave and shrewd as Gilbert Pike. Shrewd enough to follow my orders, am I not right? And you," he looked at Sheila darkly, "if you're not too spoiled by your life of pomp and power, would do well to do the same. Do with her as you see fit, lieutenant. Have the men unload the ship of its cargo and we're away."

Captain Easton swaggered across the deck while his men transferred heavy chests from the Irish ship to the pirate holds. One of the crewmen reached out for Sheila, but Gilbert Pike stopped him.

"Leave the maid to me. You'll find favor with the captain if you take that whiskey to his quarters immediately."

Then quietly, so that none could hear, Gilbert Pike bent

close to Sheila, to all appearances fixing her shawl about her. "The captain's not his usual self. There's no telling what a drinking man will do. I suggest you allow me to protect you."

"I have no need of protection. You're nothing but thieves . . . *pirates!*" She thrust the word at him like a sharp knife.

"What would you recommend? Allegiance to the crown? The queen has her own interests at heart, not those of the poor. So you're right. We've turned pirate, but as pirates we may yet find freedom. Besides," the lieutenant narrowed his eyes, "on the high seas, when a captain gives an order, the crew has but two choices: obey or mutiny."

"Freedom?" Sheila began furiously. Before she could continue, he'd picked her up and, though she struggled, managed to carry her onto the deck of the pirate ship.

"How dare you!" she cried when he released her. "My choice is to remain—"

It was too late. Peter Easton's voice bellowed the order to set sail. Sheila turned to stare at her father's ship. Captain Donahue stood at its helm. The dozen men who had chosen to remain with him were attending to the dead. The ship was quickly pulling away when suddenly Peter Easton gave another order that stopped the angry breath in Sheila's chest.

"Fire!"

No one on the pirate ship responded. Sheila turned to the lieutenant. The same horror she was feeling was reflected in his eyes.

Peter Easton let out a primitive cry of rage and thrust his sword into back of the gunman closest to him. "Fire," he yelled again. "Or shall I persuade each and every one of you?"

The gunmen sprang into action. The pirate ship let loose a volley of cannon shot hitting the Irish ship squarely at the waterline. A ragged hole appeared in the wooden timbers. Sheila heard the suck of the sea as it swept into the hold of the Irish ship, and then the cries of panic from the men on board as the ship began to tilt toward its doom.

Sheila whispered, "You call this freedom? What manner of man is your captain?"

Gilbert Pike's face was tense watching the sinking ship. "There was a time I could have answered that," he said. "The captain recently lost wife and child to the plague. He blames the queen and those in power for their deaths and the deaths of all the poor who can't escape the plague. Easton was once a loyal officer, but he's made his choice and ours too. Our lives now lie in the shadow of the gallows. I suppose he thinks the fewer witnesses, the better. And that," he stared at Sheila, "includes you."

Sheila felt a new wave of emotions: anger, relief, and in the midst of it all, a speck of pity. All too clearly, she read the frustration in Gilbert Pike's eyes. Yet he *chose* to follow this vile Captain Easton! What was the matter with men? The suitors. Her own father. And now these pirates who set men free, only to kill them.

"And you would serve such a man?"

"You say that, not understanding our choice. You've enjoyed a pampered life at court. Mine is a forced hand, a man in service. I would not choose death," Gilbert answered, watching Sheila carefully. "Would you?"

Sheila looked again at the decks of her father's ship, flooding with the sea. The last bits of her life were on that ship. She felt an unwanted sting of tears. Would she have chosen death if she had known Captain Easton meant to sink the ship? Was she so different from this man, faced with a difficult choice?

A rebellious wind gathered inside her. "You don't know

the first thing about me. I grew up as far from my father's court as he could banish me, with wise women who taught me to respect the laws and creatures of this world. I can read the sky and the wind and the soul of a person by the look in his eye. I warn you, lieutenant. Your captain will never bring you freedom. He is a lost and cruel man."

She knew she owed the lieutenant her life, yet pride controlled her. "I'll thank you not to interfere with my choices again. I would have stayed on my father's ship rather than come here with Captain Easton."

He shook his head. "You're a hard maiden to please."

"There's not a man on this boat could please me. Where are we headed?"

Gilbert Pike's voice brightened. "The captain sets our course for Newfoundland, in the New World. The fishermen are poor there and may be persuaded to join us. Captain Easton has dreams of commanding a fleet in search of riches for us all."

"New-found-land," Sheila repeated. Like the call of a songbird, the word caught her imagination. It was a lovely name.

As if he heard her thoughts, Gilbert Pike brightened and continued: "It's a lovely island, rising out of the sea, rugged and wild, with great rocky cliffs protecting narrow green inlets. The women make savory dishes with a dark red fruit called a partridge berry. Ah! Such sweetness that it tempts a man to stay on land for the rest of his life."

Sheila glanced at him sharply. Every sense in her was awake to this Gilbert Pike. The sound of his voice. That tempting smile. Worse—those clear blue eyes that promised summer.

"Newfoundland," he said, his smile wider now, "is as pleasing to the eye as the most beautiful maiden a man might hope to meet."

Sheila blushed. No man had ever spoken to her or looked at her like this. Was he playing with her? Why did he make her so confused?

"As I am homeless, it seems I must come with you, though I doubt I'll find this new land pleasing." Why was she being so contrary when everything about this land called to her?

"There are good winds. We'll have a quick journey. Allow me to show you to your cabin. There's a small one near mine. On a ship full of unpleasing pirates, you may have need of protection."

Once in her cabin, Princess Sheila walked in worried circles, thinking about her destiny and her mother's death wish. She had to be honest. The only protecting she'd need on board this ship would be from that pirate, Gilbert Pike.

JUST AS GILBERT PIKE had predicted, strong winds gave them swift passage across the Atlantic. Sheila kept to herself in her cabin, walking the deck only when she knew Captain Easton took his meals with his officers.

With each passing day, she noticed the crew gathered in small groups to talk, not the laughing banter of men taking a break, but the whispered talk of worried men, glancing covertly about them, careful whom they trusted.

One evening, while walking toward the bow, she heard wheeling gulls, calling their promise of land. Ahead, a group of men sat huddled, deep in discussion. Someone pointed at her, and the men disappeared as if they had wings. Only one remained and, before she could turn away, Gilbert Pike stood beside her.

She took a deep breath and steadied her gaze. "What is it you discuss so secretly?" she asked.

Gilbert Pike leaned close, his blue eyes lingering over the details of her face. "The men are remembering the girls they've left behind. They believe that the man who best describes the color of his true love's lips shall be a free man for the rest of his life."

He was lying, keeping the men's secrets. Yet Sheila found herself unable to answer or hold his gaze, and she looked away over the restless waves.

"You keep to yourself this voyage, princess," he continued, a bantering tone in his voice.

"It was you who advised caution on a boat full of men, was it not?"

His voice turned serious. "There *is* need for caution. Allow me to answer your question more honestly. The captain has revealed his plans. We are to raid the villages and small ships along the coast of Newfoundland. He means to force the fisherman into his service. I fear you are right about Peter Easton. I also fear that the time draws near when you must look into a man's eyes to see what lies in his heart . . . but that you will not, if he be a pirate."

His words made her shiver, as if the crones and her mother were speaking to her. Perhaps she had judged him too harshly?

"Take my cloak, princess. It has turned chilly and the cloak will keep you warm."

Before she could prevent him, he draped the cloak around her. The manly smell of Gilbert Pike rose from its every fiber, and the thick, heavy material wrapped around her body as if she were held in the very arms of the man who stood before her.

"I must go below," she said, moving away. But he walked beside her, and she was unable to remove his cloak, unable to talk, unable to think for the strange turmoil that raged inside her. As the sea roiled and the ship pitched into the deep trough of the next wave, she reached out to steady herself, finding his hand reaching out for her.

"Ahh, Sheila," he said softly, "every day, I have tried to remember the color of your lips, and now, seeing them right before me, I know they are the color of the partridge berries in Newfoundland."

She looked at his eyes and lips . . . so close she might kiss him.

Was Gilbert Pike a prince among men? How was she supposed to tell? By his lips? No. It would be wiser to trust in what her mother had wished and the crones had taught. She needed to find a new home for herself, a land of forest and sea. And if Gilbert Pike were ever to prove himself worthy, he must chose freedom before all else. She pulled away, returned him his cloak, and walked deep in thought back to her cabin.

THE NEXT MORNING, Sheila woke to find that Captain Easton had assembled the crew on deck. Gilbert Pike stood beside him, his face without expression.

"Men," Captain Easton cried, "tomorrow we will be off the coast of Newfoundland. An auspicious time to think about a new found life."

A crafty look stole over Peter Easton's face. "Think on this: why sail poor and working hard for those who are already wealthy and in power? What do we owe the queen? What has she done for us? Why not reap the spoils of the sea for ourselves?"

The men nodded amongst themselves, won over by the captain's words. Sheila pitied them. She watched Gilbert Pike. His eyes stared fixedly at the distant horizon, and his lips were set in a grim, unhappy line.

Captain Easton raised a fist in the air. "Follow me to freedom, men. We'll find plenty of poor fishermen to join us. And if they're unwilling, why, we'll persuade them with our swords. In no time, we'll have a fleet of pirates to plunder the new world. You'll be building castles and living as kings with New World slaves to serve you."

Sheila felt ill. True freedom should not depend upon the misery of others.

The captain unlocked the chest of gold that had been plundered from her father's ship. "And to prove that I'm a worthy captain and a man of his word," he flipped open the chest's lid, "I'm dividing our first spoils evenly. You'll have twenty-four hours and twenty-four pieces of gold to help you decide. If there be any here who chooses to leave tomorrow, you'll forfeit your share of gold and be put safely on the first shore we meet."

At sunset, Sheila watched the men gather, laughing and drinking, playing betting games with the gold that, for the moment, lined their pockets.

Gilbert Pike stood alone at the bow, feet spread squarely, face toward the darkening horizon. Sheila approached him, hoping he'd reveal his thoughts. He turned, a smile lighting his face.

"You are deep in thought, Gilbert Pike."

"Ahh, Sheila," he answered softly, "I have been trying to remember the color of your eyes. But I see they are as green as the hills in the new land."

"Don't mock me, Gilbert Pike. Surely there are other thoughts in your mind." Yet, standing close to him, Sheila found it hard to think of anything but the sweet promise of his eyes and the line of his lips.

Think, she ordered herself. Be careful with this strange confusion. Remember your mother's wish. . . . Ah, but if only . . . Gilbert Pike might be a prince among men.

She forced herself to ask, "Are you sure it's not the words of your captain and the direction this boat is taking tomorrow that you're contemplating?"

"I'm as sure about that, as I am about reading the clouds in the sky." He laughed bitterly. "If there be hell on water, this boat is headed there. All these weeks I've tried, but I cannot persuade the men of it. Oh no. If I am tormented—"

Again a wondrous light filled his eyes. Before she could stop him, he slipped his hand around her waist, and his breath whispered in her ear. "If I am tormented, it is at the thought of leaving you. Sheila, with lips the color of partridge berries and eyes like the hills, leave this ship with me tomorrow. I pray the land will be pleasing to your eye, and, though I cannot promise you a castle, I would make you a home. One kiss, Sheila, is all I ask."

The words of her mother's death wish coursed through every vein of her body: *not one ray of influence could she exert upon him!*

She pushed him away. "You offer your kisses the way Captain Easton bribes the men with gold. You must be faithful to your destiny," she said, turning to leave him, "and I must be faithful to mine."

Alone that night in her cabin, Princess Sheila cried as she had never cried before. Gazing into a small mirror, she contemplated her life and losses: her mother, the crones, her home in the old lost land.

And then she imagined Gilbert Pike's face in the mirror. She saw the smile on his face and the wondrous glow in his eyes as if a thousand candles were lit between them.

All that night, Sheila tossed and turned, unable to ease the ache in her heart.

"LAND HO!" came the cry of the boatswain in the morning, followed by the shouts of the men on deck.

Sheila flew from her cabin, eager to see if the land was as Gilbert Pike had described. It was an early summer morning with the sun just rising in a brilliant blue sky. She stepped on deck, shielding her eyes for a moment before she turned to gaze at the shore. They had dropped anchor close to a large island. Her heart leapt at the sight of majestic green hills atop steep rocky cliffs while the sea played in white surf at their feet.

Captain Easton stood at the bow of the boat, facing the crew. He gestured toward the island. "You see? Land. I am a man of my word. Any fool who would forfeit their share of a king's treasure—and a life of wealth with Easton's pirates—will be given safe passage there. Make your choice now or be silent."

"That's not the mainland," Gilbert cried. "The mainland of Newfoundland lies on the horizon, ten leagues away." Gilbert pointed to a dark ridge on the horizon.

"Let none say I'm not a man of my word," Captain Easton sneered. "I agreed to give safe passage to the first land we met in the morning. Well, there it be!"

"So be it," said Gilbert Pike, pulling a small bag of gold

coins from his pocket. He threw it at Captain Easton's feet. "Twenty-four pieces. I choose my freedom."

Gilbert Pike looked over the men, scanning each face slowly. "Come, men. Are there none amongst you that would join me? There's plenty of cedar on that island to build a shelter and boat. Or we'll find a fisherman to take us to the mainland, with more kindness in his heart than has our captain here. The new world offers wild, open spaces and welcoming arms for those who would be free and live an honest life."

But the men shifted their feet uneasily, shook their heads, and looked away.

Sheila's heart pounded wildly. Gilbert Pike had just forsaken a king's inheritance! He'd chosen freedom. Not a thousand, but a hundred thousand candles were lit between them.

She stepped boldly before Captain Easton. "You promised that anyone might choose to leave. That shore is more beautiful than any castle you could build. I will leave with Gilbert Pike. Keep my father's gold, and may God save you all."

Captain Easton's face flooded red with rage. Sheila had trapped him in his word.

Gilbert Pike stepped beside her and reached his arms behind her waist. "In appearance this island resembles the mainland. I take it you find it pleasing," he said, not caring who might hear.

Behind Gilbert stood the high, magnificent cliffs, a natural castle fit to call home. Sheila looked into Gilbert Pike's eyes and steadily met his gaze.

"It is a land most pleasing to my eye. But you, Gilbert Pike, are even more so."

"Then kiss me, Sheila. Your mouth is the color of—"

Sheila stopped him. His lips were wondrously close, and

she wasn't going to let another second pass with more than a breath between them.

Historical Note

Very little is known about Sheila NaGeira, legendary princess of Newfoundland. She and Gilbert Pike arrived safely on the mainland, where they married and lived many happy years until their village was attacked. Sheila led the village women in protecting their children. The men were slaughtered or, like Gilbert, taken prisoner by none other than the dreaded pirate, Peter Easton.

It took years to rebuild the community. Sheila was loved and respected by all, wooed by many. But she remained faithful in her love for Gilbert Pike, choosing to wait for him to return.

Fifteen long years passed before Gilbert managed to escape and make his way back to Newfoundland and Sheila. There, just as the crones had foreseen and her mother had wished, they lived a free and happy life together until their natural deaths.

Far from Home: Marie Robichaud's Journal

December 24, 1755, on The Sally

THIS JOURNAL MAY PROVE to be my godsend. Strangely, it was my enemy, the English captain, who gave it to me.

To be fair, Captain Franklin does what he can to ease our suffering. Tonight he said he could not allow us to celebrate our Christmas mass, claiming he was under orders to not tolerate papist witchcraft. But under his breath he added, "What goes on below deck is naught of my affair."

I know he pities us. I saw his face the day we boarded *The Sally*, the day they forced us from Grand-Pré, so many weeks ago. That's when he gave me pen and paper.

My memory of that day is all confused, as if I had been in a fevered state. What happened first? I cannot separate the sight of our homes, burning in the distance, from the sight of my beloved husband, François, dead in my arms. I remember dragging him into our house—or was it out?

Someone must have found me, holding François outside our burning home after the soldiers killed him. I must have lost consciousness, for the next thing I knew I was standing beside Maman on the deck of *The Sally,* leaving the bay, watching the smoke of Grand-Pré—and no doubt, François—mingle with the clouds.

The first week onboard, I was so ill from the motion of the sea I could not rise from my narrow place in the hold. The ice on the walls was several inches thick, and I dreamt I was in a palace of ice. François' spirit met me there and spoke to me often. He told me I would make a home elsewhere, to the north of Grand-Pré, but that he was at peace because he'd died in our home; he could not have tolerated being a prisoner of the English.

One day at last I awoke, and the rocking of the ship was a thing outside of me, not inside me. I will never forget that terrible dizziness. How good it felt to stand and walk the deck, though I was weak and had to hold the gunwales to keep from falling. The captain bid me good morning and asked what he could do for me. That's when I asked for pen and paper, feeling a weight upon my heart and not knowing how else to set it down. Maman is so burdened, I dare not ask her for comfort. She gets a pained look, and I know she is thinking of Papa, wondering if he is still in prison in Halifax, or on a boat like this one bound for a port unknown. Either way, we are separated by the English and the sea.

At midnight, we celebrated mass quietly in the hold. We have no priest. The English sent him on a boat to France. They hope that without a priest we will not keep our faith. But we asked for God's blessing over the wine and bread and confessed our sins anyway. I am filled with hatred for the English, especially for the soldiers who killed François. It is like nothing I have ever known before, this hatred. It rages inside me worse than the winter storm outside that whips the sea and tosses this ship, heaving like a mother cow that cannot bear its backwards calf. It is a destruction that will kill me if it remains inside. I ask God to take it from me.

Antoine Poirier is on our ship. He keeps a distance from me, I think, and avoids conversation. He knows François is dead. Maybe he never forgave me for marrying François instead of him. Otherwise, I cannot fathom the reason for his distance. Or perhaps he's separated on these cursed boats from a love that bloomed last summer before the English imprisoned the men. Perhaps he suffers unreasonably, as I do when I cannot put François from my mind.

Yesterday, Thérèse found the fiddle. She begged me to bring it out so that there could be dancing and music, but I scolded her. I told her the priests were right. The fiddle is an instrument of the devil. François insisted on trying to save it from our burning house, and it cost him his life. All these days and nights, I've kept the thing wrapped in my old shawl, hidden away. It lies beside me instead of François, and the twisted strings call out to me with memories.

I could do as Thérèse asks and give the thing to Antoine. Then we would have music to lighten our hearts, and I would be rid of it. I should do this for Maman and Thérèse, for Gilles and Pierre—for everyone. But God forgive me, I can't!

January 15, 1756, on The Sally
TOMORROW WE ARRIVE in Jamestown, Virginia. The captain assures us that the land is plentiful and good, anything can grow there. He calls it a land blessed by its Christian men and women. Ah! But will these Christians share their blessings with French Catholics?

One of the seamen told us of the great plantations and

how they grow tobacco, a plant that grows low to the ground. It breaks the back to pick it all day. They bring ships full of black men, women, and children from Africa. They are all separated and sold as slaves to these great plantations. I look at Maman and Thérèse, Gilles and Pierre, and I pray to God that this will not be our destiny—to break our backs as French slaves for English landowners.

The stench in the hold of the ship where we sleep is unbearable. Though we have been careful to ration food and fresh water, already six people have died. Every day I fear that Thérèse or Gilles or Pierre will not get up, but lie weak and sick in the hold like those who have died. At night, the coughing in the hold never stops. Thérèse whimpers that she cannot sleep. I stuff bits of cloth in her ears to block the sound, and I hold her close to keep us warm. It helps. Maman lies beside me, holding Pierre and Gilles. I remember Grand-Pré and the wind brushing the golden hair of our fields. I listen to the wind and creaking of the timbers, and I imagine François' arms around me, like the sea. And then I dream.

January 16, 1756, on The Sally, *Jamestown, Virginia*
WITH THE DAWN'S LIGHT, we arrive in the harbor and drop anchor. Captain Franklin told us that he carries letters from Colonel Winslow to the governor here, Robert Dinwiddie. Winslow begs the inhabitants' kind assistance in resettling us in Virginia.

Across the water, I watch the captain's red coat disappear amongst the port's shadowy buildings. People are starting to bustle about. What looks like a small market sits at the water's edge, and plain farm folk are coming with their carts to trade and sell their goods. I hear the sounds of the English language across the water, and am glad I have learned some words. I will have need of them in this new land. I see none of the dark-skinned slaves we heard about. Perhaps the sailor exaggerated.

The widow Leblanc is also up.

"Land!" she cries, a huge smile on her face. We are all eager to get off the ship. To feel the earth beneath our feet. To bathe. To eat a good, hot meal.

Mme. Leblanc has lost so much weight this past month, her clothes flap long and loose about her. Of all our neighbors, she is the one most changed. Yesterday, I helped her sew new seams and tucks in her good skirt, as she feared for her appearance in what will be our new home. "Always hold your head high, Marie," she told me. "Put your best dress on."

We laughed at that. It was good to laugh. We each have only one good dress amongst our few belongings.

We are lucky to have the silver Maman remembered to bring. I have sewn some of it into the hem of my one good dress and some into the shawl. Like so many of our neighbors, Mme. Leblanc was sure she would return to Grand-Pré one day, and she left her valuables buried in a corner of her fruit cellar. Only when we watched the soldiers torch our homes, even our church, only when we knelt on the decks of *The Sally* and saw the smoke of Grand-Pré mingle with the clouds in the distance, only then did everyone realize that Grand-Pré was gone. It lives only as a memory now.

Mme. Leblanc brought food instead of valuables, and to our amazement she has shared it with all, even the dying. Maman says it is God's hand at work. If Maman has hope, then I must too.

Maman says that when we get off this vessel, when we

have a roof over our heads and a field to plant and a few animals, then we will start again.

January 17, 1756, on The Sally, *Jamestown, Virginia*
A TERRIBLE DAY. Captain Franklin returns to the ship. His face is long and hard as he tells us the news. "You arrive unannounced and unwanted. Colonel Winslow's letter is the first they have heard of your coming here."

He has difficulty continuing. When he finds it difficult to speak, he has a way of swallowing many times. "You are French. You are papists. They will not allow you to disembark."

I look across the water at the town, the farmers milling about the open market. The women wear long skirts and bonnets much like ours, yet they fear us. We have no home and carry but a few belongings allowed by the English. All we need is a little land, a marshy scrap they don't use. But they fear our language and religion.

A group is gathering on the dock. They stare at us and talk amongst themselves. One of them, a tall man, raises his fist and yells something. I can't make it out. The others raise their fists too, and they all begin to yell. They are yelling at us!

Some of them bend to pick up things. Rocks. They hurl the rocks toward us. The rocks splash into the water. I step back and hold Thérèse close, though I know the rocks cannot reach us.

Pierre and Gilles run away from Maman. Their faces are angry and they are searching for something on the deck. I look back at the crowd growing larger and larger on the waterfront. More and more rocks fly through the air toward us. Gilles and Pierre find soup bones in a bucket and start to fling them toward the townspeople, but Captain Franklin stops them.

"You'll have to learn to take it, boys," he orders them gruffly. "You'll only make things worse if you fight back."

I'm glad François is not here to see our shame. He would tell my brothers to fight for all they are worth. He would fling more than a bucket; he'd turn the guns upon these Virginians.

Antoine Poirier takes my brothers to the far side of the deck. He puts an arm about their shoulders, talking to them the way Papa would, if only he were here. Their heads hang low as they listen but finally they nod reluctantly.

Antoine catches me staring at him. I smile, hoping to show the gratitude I feel. But he turns away and my smile is lost in the twists and turns of the rigging that ropes its way up the mast of this English ship.

January 19, 1756, on The Sally, *Jamestown, Virginia*
YESTERDAY ANOTHER VESSEL anchored beside us.

"It's a slaver from Africa," one of the seamen told us.

We watched as a heavy door covering the hold was thrown open. Before we saw them, we heard them.

We heard the harsh scraping of metal chains. One by one, people crawled out of the hold of the slave ship. It was a bright, sunny day and they shielded their eyes as they stumbled in their restrictive chains. I could not breathe as I watched them. They were bound to one another at the ankles. I was filled with a rage so wild, I feared I would lose my senses.

I must have cried out, for Maman took hold of my hand and pressed it hard.

"What has happened to the world?" I asked her.

"I don't know," she said. I've never known Maman without a long explanation for the events of this world.

We were silent, watching their misery. It violated our senses. We could smell the dark-skinned people's fear as they were lowered into longboats. They were taken to shore, to the market. Crowds of townsfolk gathered in front of the market. Captain Franklin said they began with the children, then the women, and finally the strong, young men. One by one, they were auctioned off. When we heard wailing, we knew mothers were separated from their children.

I could not pretend to be an adult any longer. I clung to Maman, just as Pierre, Gilles, and Thérèse did, as if Maman had wings to fold around us. I felt ashamed, yet could not stop my prayer.

"Please, God. Don't let it happen to us."

January 25, 1756, on The Sally, *Jamestown, Virginia*
THEY ARE SENDING US to England. Two small vessels are being readied with provisions for the journey. Tomorrow we are to divide into two groups and board them.

I ask Gilles about his agreement with Antoine Poirier, on the day of the rock throwing. He speaks bitterly. Antoine cautioned him that the English have power over us; we are their prisoners. We will not survive if we fight back. It is neither the time nor the way. We must be patient and outwait them. In the future they will have new enemies and they will forget about us. Then we will go back to Acadia, find a place that is safe from the English, and we will build new homes.

That Antoine. He is so much like Papa, calm and able to reason in any situation, so unlike the fiery passion in François. I could not help but love François and choose him, though I understand better now why Papa used to caution me: fire in a man burns a dangerous path and is unable to contain itself.

Gilles tells me, in a voice as harsh as flint, that he has agreed not to fight back. He is a boy. An angry boy.

"It is a good plan for us," I argue. Gilles worshipped François, and it is an opportunity to speak to that love. "It is exactly what François said would happen if the English managed to steal Grand-Pré. In the land to the north of Acadia, we must rebuild our new homes. The English don't want that land. They won't destroy us there. Can you imagine, if we all make our way back and—"

Tears stop me. Only in my dreams would François say such a thing. Fighting was his nature. To urge compromise in this way is desperation, but it is all we have.

"—and meet Papa."

Gilles does not laugh at me. Tears well in his eyes, the first I have seen there. We hug fiercely, vowing to stay together.

"No matter what," he says, "we'll go back to the land north of Grand-Pré."

Such a crazy dream. But how good to hold my brother close and know we share it.

January 31, 1756, on The Prosperous

THE WORST HAS HAPPENED. We are separated.

Maman and Thérèse and I were lowered off *The Sally* in a longboat, with all our belongings, to be rowed to one of the two waiting vessels. Gilles and Pierre were still on deck above us with Mme. Leblanc when she remembered the cook, who'd taken quite a fancy to her. He'd given her an old iron pot he did not need. Gilles and Pierre went off to help her carry it, but the seaman on deck assumed we were ready and untied us from *The Sally*. The next thing we knew, we were pulling away and another longboat was taking our place to load those remaining on *The Sally*.

Maman and I protested, begged the rowers to turn back, but none of them spoke French. I pointed to the deck of *The Sally* and shouted in English, "My brothers!" The rowers looked and nodded and spoke among themselves . . . but they did not turn back.

Gilles and Pierre and Mme. Leblanc climbed into the waiting longboat. All the while we were growing farther and farther apart, but we assumed they would follow us.

The other longboat did not follow us. When I saw that it was headed for the second vessel, I felt as helpless as a fish caught in a net. So many struggles, always trapped. We were separated yet again. We were hurried onboard this new vessel. The captain was too busy to listen to us, and when he finally did, it was too late. The other ship had already lifted anchor and set sail.

"No matter," the captain assured Maman. She was hit harder by this separation than by the one from Grand-Pré. She collapsed on her knees before him, but he laughed at her concerns. "You'll find them in England. You're *all* going to England."

He is an ugly man, with warts across his forehead and the bright flush of one who drinks too much, and often.

Antoine—dear man!—gathered Maman into his arms, assuring her that the boys would be well protected by Mme. Leblanc on their voyage. "You know Giselle. She has a knack of getting her way," he joked, making Maman smile faintly. "We will meet them in England, healthy and fat."

All we can do is pray. I am thankful Antoine is with us.

This vessel is not so crowded as *The Sally*. It is named *The Prosperous*. I do not understand the meaning of its name, but I hope that it is something that bodes well for our future. Once we are in England, we must petition the King of France to save us. He will hear our pleas, for this time we will be close enough to shout across the sea to gain his attention.

May 3, 1756, on The Prosperous

WE ARE ONLY ONE DAY AWAY from the shores of England. The captain told us recently the name of our destination: Bristol. This word is hard to pronounce.

The voyage has been long, and we are down to the last of our provisions. Antoine has looked to our needs every day. We are on speaking terms, though he makes sure never to be alone with me. Only once did this happen, by accident, yesterday, when we happened to see the dead seaman.

I was lost in my thoughts near the stern of the ship when I saw the body. It was wrapped in a blanket and carried upon a plank, about to be tipped into the sea. There was something furtive in the sailors' hurried movements. Antoine came up behind me, motioning me to keep quiet. We watched the wind tease the blanket from the corpse. The man's upper body was covered in strange, red blisters, like pimples. Antoine pulled me away before we were noticed.

"What is it?" I whispered.

"The pox."

My heart stopped. We never suffered the pox in Grand-Pré. Everyone knows to fear it, knows it spreads and kills with the fury of a storm.

"Why do they try to hide it from us?"

"There will be panic on the ship if everyone finds out. And

there is nothing we can do to prevent it once it starts. We can only hope that it will not break out before the end of our voyage."

"Perhaps it is an isolated case. Oh, but this voyage cannot end too soon."

I nearly reached out to take his hand as we shared the terrible discovery that the pox was on the ship with us. But I could not touch him; my own secret prevented me. We agreed to keep this worry to ourselves and not alarm the others. None amongst us have that sickness yet—have we not endured enough!—and when I catch Antoine's eye, I know he is as anxious as I am now to set foot on England's soil, strange though it seems.

I am eager to be off this ship, for I have my own secret, though this one is joyous. I am with child, François' child. God has answered my prayers. My monthlies do not come. My belly swells like a mainsail in the wind, and I am filled with hope. I have not told Maman. I will wait until we are on ground, safely, with a roof over our heads and reunited with Gilles and Pierre.

We will not be struck down by the pox. We will be a family again, and we will survive these trials to build a new Acadia. I feel a need to celebrate, if only to bring us better luck. And so I have given Antoine the fiddle, and for the first time, there is music and dancing. It is good to see my little sister laugh.

This is our last night on board *The Prosperous*. I sleep more easily. Again I dream of François, but tonight he smiles. He stands by the shores of Grand-Pré, waving to me while the wind rocks our child, our future, to sleep.

One Mighty Kiss

On a farm outside Regina, Nellie MacKinnon, sixteen,
prepares for the Gala Ball of 1891. She'll be escorted by
Officer Fitzhenry of the North West Mounted Police.
Fitzhenry is her father's choice, polished boots, every inch
the man of law and order.

Late afternoon Nellie bathes,
shadowy waters of the coulee.
She dives and floats, imagines strange figures
in the prairie clouds above.
Swimming to shore she discovers
her clothes are not on the rock
where she left them.
Behind the trunk of a willow
her dress appears
in the hand of Jean-Pierre, eighteen,
Pa's hired help.
Last week under yellow stooks of wheat
he told her stories of his people—
buffalo hunts and Louis Riel,

hated by eastern Canada,

hung by John A. Macdonald.

Riel paid attention to visions. A voice inspired

his fight for independence,

a little Metis corner of North West prairie.

That Jean-Pierre—

those dark, laughing eyes,

his soft lips she's been thinking about all summer.

Treading water, she orders,

"Put my clothes back on the rock!"

"Can't do that. I got a voice inspiring me."

Says you should come out here,

get them yourself, *chérie.*"

She splashes him. "I'll get my pa to fire you!"

Jean-Pierre winks,

pulls his bandana over his eyes.

"Ici, chérie."

The water slips along her hot, parched skin.

She's never felt so confused.

Stay in or get out?

"Jean-Pierre . . . if I weren't a girl . . . oh, the things I would
do to you!"

"But you're a girl, *Dieu merci,* and—oh!—the things you do
to me!"

She glares,

this Metis boy! this Mighty boy!

"That voice better tell you to keep your eyes shut!"

She runs from the water, grabs her clothes, ready to flee . . .

but is stopped by a vision in the vast prairie sky:

The ghost of John A. Macdonald staggers west, carried by
hundreds of balloons.[1]

Brown from buffalo hunts and the sun,
Jean-Pierre's hands reach out,
calluses like closed eyes
keeping a promise.
"Nellie, I'll close my eyes for *toujours* if you'll kiss me, just
    one kiss."
Her eyes slide along
the slow curve of his lips.
Jean-Pierre, a new world,
nothing like Officer Fitzhenry.
"Well . . . maybe . . . if you put your hands behind your
    back . . ."
Poof! hands disappear.
One step closer . . .
two . . .
she kisses him.
His lips
wet and sweet;
it's like drinking
heavenly
water.
After the ball, Officer Fitzhenry escorts Nellie home.
He tells her he's asked her pa for her hand in marriage.
He boasts he'll be able to support a wife with his new post-
    ing in northern Alberta.
Could he kiss her?
Over his shoulder she sees another vision in the immense
    night sky:
A herd of buffalo chases John A. east, off the fields of the moon.
Well, she thinks,
a Mountie deserves an equal opportunity—

it's more than they gave Riel.[2]
Fitzhenry is so tall
she has to crick her neck back.
His thin lips press rigidly,
the very tools of law and order.
His red jacket scratches
her thirsty skin.
Her eyes fly open. It only takes a second
to wipe him off her lips.
In the courtroom of the heart, it's a landmark decision:
Officer Fitzhenry just lost his woman to a kiss.

[1] Sir John A. Macdonald, the first Prime Minister of Canada, was famous for his enjoyment of alcohol and for thinking up new ways to travel west.

[2] In 1885, Louis Riel was tried for treason in Regina by a jury of six white Anglo-Saxon Protestants, found guilty, and executed. He received a full pardon in 1991.

Badlands

FUNNY, how a letter can change your life. A year ago last June, Mama read her sister's most recent letter, and her face dried up hard as the earth in a drought. She folded Aunt Mathilda's words deep into her pocket, then went into her room "to lie down." Usually, she'd pass a letter directly to me, and I'd read it aloud to the family after dinner. Aunt Mathilda's news always gave us something to talk about other than the cows and the weather, or the tattletaling amongst my younger brothers. But a whole week passed before Mama gave me that letter. I unfolded it nervously, reading the last lines of my aunt's energetic scrawl with an excitement that had no place to grow beside my mother's reaction.

> *Drumheller needs a new teacher for September. It's*
> *partly a result of the train, bringing surveyors looking*
> *for coal and ranchers wanting open spaces. The West*
> *seems to be charging toward the end of the nineteenth*
> *century without any brakes on. Last week, two groups*
> *of scientists arrived from Ottawa and New York.*
> *Imagine, all the way down east they know about Mr.*

Tyrrell's discoveries in the badlands. In town we call it
a Dinosaur Rush.

    I know Sybil's your only daughter, well behaved and
female company to you, but it's an opportunity for her.
She's eighteen and has her own future to think about.
You could hire a local girl to help you. Think on it. It
would open Sybil's eyes to the world.
Love to all,
Mathilda

I finished reading and looked at Mama. Her eyes appeared
fixed on something outside the window, some bit of bad
weather as troublesome as Aunt Mathilda's suggestion.

"I won't leave," I assured her. How could I abandon her to
our chaotic, male-dominated home? I had six younger brothers who worked the ranch with Papa. When they were inside
we couldn't string two thoughts together to spell peace or
quiet.

Mama's fatigue had been a gradual thing, but it got notice-
ably worse after Daniel, the youngest, was born six years ago.
That's when she started going back to bed after breakfast. I
blamed it on the boys. Six boys was six too many. If I didn't
clean up their morning mess, it'd still be there at noon when
they clomped inside with their dirty boots, pushing and
bawling like crazed cows over who got to eat what first, every
one of them hollering. Then they'd clomp out again, leaving
me and Mama staring dazed after their footprints, just like
we'd been stampeded.

The doctor came once and declared Mama "plumb tuckered out." I could have told anybody that for the asking.

All summer Aunt Mathilda's words rolled around in my

head, drifting and bumping against my thoughts like a loosened clump of tumbleweed: *open Sybil's eyes to the world.* I was always borrowing books, itching to see things, meet new people and ideas. If I stayed at home, I feared my fate: becoming a rancher's wife like Mama.

Aunt Mathilda had married a man who worked for the CPR. She was a knowledgeable and well-traveled woman, the head of a hundred committees, and, unlike the farmers' wives I knew, she had no children. No one kept her up nights sick, wore out their belongings in a week, or got into scraps with the neighbors—man or beast. When I asked Mama why Aunt Mathilda had no children, she said it was because Uncle Ross was away so much. He didn't demand "wifely duties."

"What's that mean exactly?"

Mama answered the way a barncat chases its tail, "Givin' him children."

I knew darn well the biological workings of procreation. I'd seen it on the farm hundreds of times, the heated act of mating. Sometimes female cats had so many litters, they plain and simple disappeared. I'd find their thin, wasted skeletons and knew that life had been procreated right out of them.

"Can't a woman say no?"

We were kneeling in Mama's garden at the time. My last question resulted in a vigorous yanking of a deep-rooted weed from the ground.

"Marriage is complicated," Mama answered, holding up the weed with a grim smile. "And nature has a way of interfering." She sighed heavily and sat back on her heels. "Maybe you *should* go to Drumheller like Mathilda suggested. Find yourself a husband who works for the rails."

Had I heard right? Was this the opportunity to escape that

might never present itself again? I fetched two pails to water Mama's nasturtiums, her favorite flower. In the fall, she harvested their seeds and planted them around the well, the road, everywhere she liked.

"Do you mean it, Mama? You wouldn't mind if I went?" I passed her a hopeful pail.

Mama kept her head down, pouring trickles of water around the green shoots. "I didn't say *that*. But if you mean to go, best arrange it quick."

I dropped my pail and ran into the house. I'd already been delayed by second thoughts. I wasn't going to let third ones stop me. I wrote Aunt Mathilda a note saying I'd come teach for a year in Drumheller, rode our fastest horse into town to post it, and the thing was done.

I thought Mama might be pleased and proud when I was offered the position, but when the time came to leave at the end of August, she refused to come to the train station to see me off. Papa and the boys sat out in the wagon waiting while I tried to say good-bye. She lay in bed, her face averted. The hunched line of her back accused me plain as day: *I didn't want this.*

With her face to the wall, she might have been dead. How badly I wanted to hug and kiss her, but I didn't know how, not when she'd closed herself off like that. I lacked something around Mama—courage or maturity, I never knew what. Some part of me was always a little girl, tiptoeing close, bringing her wildflowers and kisses, ineffectively trying to make her happy.

"Bye, Mama," I whispered. "I'll write."

Outside, the boys were fighting on the wagon, pushing one another off, Papa yelling at them to behave lest they wanted a whupping.

Driving up the hill, my thoughts wheeled over and over. My great adventure had a price. Should I run back, try to take better care of her? How could I leave her like that? The wagon kicked up dust behind us. I fixed my eyes on the house. Maybe she'd appear at the window. What if she raised her arm to beckon me back? I stood up to see more clearly.

The dust swirled up between us in a blinding cloud, and Daniel yanked me back down in my seat.

IF I'D THOUGHT home and cleaning up after six brothers was punishment, my first day of teaching was hell. I had twenty students of all ages. Eighteen of them were boys. Aunt Mathilda had neglected to mention the part about them running the last three teachers out of town.

That first morning I was sure Mama had prayed for such a calamity to bring me home. Looking over my classroom, spitballs and insults flying, hands smacking, bodies bouncing, I nearly gave up. Then the image of my mother lying in bed, head turned away, loomed before me.

No! I wouldn't give up without a fight.

I thought of the punishment my brothers had hated the most at school, and I smacked the ruler as hard as I could across my desk. Thwack! I commanded an astonished silence.

"Before I came here I was offered six teaching positions in eastern Canada where I'm told boys are better behaved." I *knew* western pride. "It's up to you. Do I stay? Or leave on the next train?"

I glared at them. They gaped back.

"*If* I stay, we agree to the rules right now. No doubt, you're familiar with writing lines."

A huge groan rose from every male throat.

"Fine. I'll set other punishments that will be fair and appropriate. Those of you who cannot agree . . . can go home right now."

On the board, I wrote:

<u>Speaking out of turn</u>: chopping the teacher's wood

<u>Fighting</u>: bringing in the teacher's water and cleaning her dishes

<u>Bloody fighting</u>: cleaning the privy

<u>Bad language</u>: cleaning out the teacher's cabin and stove.

Miraculously, the boys accepted the new rules, grateful I had not imposed the most worthless, meaningless, tedious insult known to boys: the writing of lines. After my first week as teacher in Drumheller, I sat down to a clean house. I hadn't washed a dish all week. The woodpile was enormous. I felt pleased with myself and found the courage to write my mother a long letter, eager to relate to her as one woman to another. I imagined her sitting up in bed, excited to hear my news.

Dearest Mama,

I arrived safely and survived my first week. How about you? I'm hoping you were able to hire Agathe St. Denis to help you.

There is a Metis boy in my class here, Roland Pelletier, who reminds me of her and, come to think of it, of Daniel. Roland is the same age as Daniel and has the same big eyes. He loves stories too, both the telling and the hearing. The first day, I shared my lunch with him and he told me about his grandfather who was a buffalo hunter. I told him about my train trip,

*crossing mile after mile of prairie and how it looked like
an ocean. I told him how you traveled across
Saskatchewan as a little girl on a Red River cart and
how a Metis family helped Grandpa ford the
Saskatchewan River. Mama, remember how you'd say,
"And they told Grandpa a great secret: if you knotted
the horse's tail and lashed a buffalo-hide rope from the
cart to the horse's tail, the horse could pull the cart
across the river with his tail."*

*Roland loved that part. "You mean your grandpa
didn't know that?"*

*I have eighteen wild boys in my classroom. I wonder
if there's a secret to surviving this year? I'll need the
strength of a horse's tail to manage them.*

*I saw my first buffalo outside the train window.
Roland was quite excited about that too. The buffalo
are gone here with all the settlement and hunting. I
guess they had nowhere to hide on this ocean. That
buffalo was magnificent with its dark shaggy fur, mas-
sive shoulders, and bearded head. He ran right beside
the track, and I imagined hundreds more around, stam-
peding. Wouldn't that have been a sight!*

*But the worst thing happened. The man behind me
stood up and yelled, "Buffalo!" He grabbed his rifle
from under his seat, ran to the end of our cabin and into
the next, the caboose. All the while I watched the solitary buffalo, willing it to run away, but it seemed bent
on racing us. I saw a tiny explosion in the earth near
him. I banged on the window to warn him. Maybe he
heard me. He veered from the train but another bullet
hit his backside. His hind legs gave out and he collapsed*

*into the ground, red blood gushing everywhere. His head
rose one last time above the grass, then sank again.
When the gunman came back into the cabin, the other
passengers cheered and clapped him on the shoulder.*

"Nice shooting."

*I don't think I've ever felt so strange, as if I might
be a different species from people around me. Especially
that man. What could we possibly have in common?*

*I felt lonely until I shared this story with Roland.
Angry tears came to his eyes as they did to mine.*
"Why did the man kill it? He didn't need it."

"They call it sport," I answered.

*Mama, I don't think I'll ever marry, not even a
man who is away a lot.*

Your loving daughter,
Sybil

While my thoughts about love and marriage plummeted
that first month, I instinctively found the secret to good
teaching. I respected my students; they respected me back.
We read. We talked. We studied the world together. It was
much like pouring water on my mother's nasturtiums.

Then, one Sunday in early October, I met one of the pale-
ontologists at church and made several other startling discoveries.

"John Crossing," he introduced himself. "You're the new
teacher from Saskatchewan."

I'd seen him from a distance other Sundays. I liked the way
his dark curls clung neatly to his head. He had an intelligent,
open face that gazed directly at a person when he was listening. When he approached me over tea after the service, he

walked with the slow rhythm of a man who trusted his physical strength but didn't need to flaunt it. His skin was tanned from long days outside. His brown eyes were clear—perfect eyes for a scientist—drawing conclusions about everything around him. I knew he'd been watching me. Had I met his approval?

"And you're from New York? A museum?" I wasn't sure how to pronounce *paleontologist* and didn't risk it.

"Natural history." There was a hypnotic drawl to his speech. "The whole town's talking about you. Half the size of your students, and you've got them cleaning your dishes, eating out of your hand. You must feel right at home in the badlands."

"Badlands?" I laughed at the associations that word provided and, because he'd so aptly found a word that uncovered my feelings, I confided, "That word describes my whole life, past and present."

He raised his eyebrows, wanting to know more.

"I grew up with six wild brothers, but even so, that class of mine was an awful shock."

He laughed. "Tried to escape your past, did you? It always comes back to haunt you, one way or another. I did something like that myself coming out here. I'm a banker's son with no interest in money. My father doesn't approve of my digging up bones. He calls it a dog's life."

I smiled at his puns, drawn to the way he poked fun at himself. "My brothers were always tearing around, teasing, thinking up pranks, and I thought I'd get away from—"

But I couldn't continue. I missed them! In my mind I saw clearly the hunched line of a woman's back. It wasn't my brothers I needed distance from. It was my mother.

My voice trailed, unable to reveal all this to a complete stranger. "But I guess my brothers aren't so bad."

"I heard you got the boys in line like no teacher has managed yet." He spoke and looked at me so directly that I blushed.

"It's amazing how helpful boys can be when you appeal to their interests directly."

"Maybe you'd like to bring your class out to the site for a natural history lesson. Extinction might appeal to them."

My face must have been a question.

"It's a powerful notion, extinction. Didn't you ever wonder what happened to the dinosaurs? They ruled the earth sixty-five million years ago. And now they're gone. What circumstances could make that happen to us, humans? There are powerful forces affecting us all the time. . . ."

Something else appeared in his eyes, not just intelligence and wit. Some new force made us stop talking and just look and smile at each other.

"Come out to the site. Please. I'd like to see you again."

The next week was unusually fair. Late Monday morning John Crossing arrived at school with a wagon and invited us for an outdoor class in natural history. I looked at the class sternly, as if my heart wasn't racing, pretending to consider.

"Hmm. Nathan, Joseph, Edward. Are your sums corrected?"

"Yes, miss."

"Roland. Can you run to my cabin and pack two dozen apples—how many is that?"

Roland squealed with delight, "Twenty-four, miss!"

It was a huge success. John was a fine teacher, passionate about uncovering secrets in the layered rocks. And I was relieved to have something to write home about. I hadn't been able to write since receiving Mama's only letter:

> *Dear Sybil,*
> *Fall is here. I saved my nasturtium seeds, labeled them*
> *in different envelopes according to color. I hope I have*
> *more energy to plant them next spring. I am pregnant*
> *again. The baby is due in April or early May. Hope*
> *you are well. We read your letters every evening and*
> *they are a comfort.*
> *Love,*
> *Mama*

Riding in John Crossing's wagon, I sat up front beside him while the class chattered happily in the back. With those scientist's brown eyes, he observed my unvoiced fear.

"You seem worried, Sybil."

"My mother's pregnant."

"That's not good news?"

"Oh no. It's the worst thing imaginable. My little brother Daniel was supposed to be the last. It's understood in the family. My mother can't manage another child, the way she is."

There was an odd silence between us. An expected child was usually the cause for joy. I didn't feel I could say more without betraying my mother's private state. I turned my head to read the expression on John's face, needing to know if he were sympathetic or critical. His eyes met mine kindly.

"You're close to your mother, aren't you?"

I burst into tears. All talking ceased in the back of the wagon. Roland crawled forward and put his small, grubby hand on the sleeve of my dress.

"Are you all right, miss?"

What a question. If I tried to answer it, there was nowhere to start or end. I couldn't tell him that, no, I wasn't all right, that my mother was like a barn cat, exhausted from too many pregnancies, from life, every bit as dried up as these badlands around us lying all hunched up beside what was left of the riverbed and—oh, it just went on and on, nowhere. I needed a word for it and didn't know one that was adequate.

I held Roland's hand gratefully. "It's my mother. She's . . . ill."

After the day spent with John Crossing and my students in the badlands, I felt cheered enough to respond to Mama's letter.

> *Dear Mama,*
>
> *I've made a new friend, John Crossing, a paleontologist from the Museum of Natural History in New York. He studies ancient life by looking at their remains. He's part of the dinosaur rush here. The Geological Survey of Canada is pitted against the Americans in the search for dinosaur bones.*
>
> *John took my class to his site, where we learned about fossils. The badlands are steep, dry valleys following the Red Deer River for miles. You stand at the top of flat prairie land, and then you look down at a desert gorge carved out by the river. John says the sides are layers of sandstone, mudstone, coal, and shale. Joseph Tyrrell found the first dinosaur bone here ten years ago, the skull of a seventy-million-year-old carnivore.*
>
> *John Crossing is going back to New York for the winter, but he will return in May to take us to his new*

> *site. I am looking forward to studying more with him.*
> *I'm also looking forward to holding the new baby*
> *when I come home for the summer.*
> *Your loving daughter,*
> *Sybil*

It was the best I could do without lying. I did like to hold babies. I just wished my mother wasn't having one.

My mother wrote back:

> *John Crossing sounds even better than a man who*
> *works for the rails.*

Not once in our correspondence that winter did we mention *plumb tuckered out*. Neither did I mention how I kissed John Crossing when he left, nor how long I found the months without him. He sent me an amber necklace for Christmas with a note explaining that amber was the fossilized resin of ancient trees known as "tears of the gods." In Greek mythology, Zeus transformed the daughters of the sun god into poplar trees after they wept for a dead sibling. Their tears hardened and fell to the ground as amber.

I wore that amber necklace every day while the snowdrifts grew as high as poplar trees. It hardly seemed possible anything green would survive to grow from the hard, frozen earth. Spring would never come again.

But it did. And with it came a letter from home. I picked it up from the post office at the back of the general store. When I saw Papa's childish, awkward printing on the strange, lumpy envelope, my hand started to shake. A cold, clammy dread spread down my face and neck. Papa never read or wrote anything. It was Mama who wrote the letters. I fumbled with the envelope, pulling it open in the middle of the store.

> *Dear Sybil,*
> *Mama died in childbirth. So did the baby, a girl. When the ground thaws we will bury them at the end of the garden. She wanted you to have her seeds.*
> *Papa*

Several ladies took me home, made me tea, and put me to bed. The whole town must have found out. On Monday morning, my students came early to clean the classroom and chop wood, stacking the woodpile so high there was enough to keep a fire burning for at least another year.

I walked in, unable to meet my students' eyes. I went to the chalkboard and gave them their instructions:

> *Good morning. Thank-you for being here. I can't talk yet. Please get out your journals and write things you wish you could say to your mother, but can't for some reason.*

I sat at my desk and composed my last letter.

> *Dear Mama,*
> *Now you're the one who's gone, but where? I can't stop thinking about our last good-bye. I wish I'd kissed you. I tell myself I could never have saved you, but it does-n't help. Thank-you for sending me your seeds. I will plant them soon as the ground has thawed and I will harvest the seeds every fall the way you did. I want to*

stay here another year, maybe more. Whatever I lacked
as a daughter, I'm a good teacher. I have found the
strength of a horse's tail.

John Crossing returned in May. There was so much turmoil inside me that I couldn't tell him how much I'd missed
him. He didn't press me to talk, just asked me to go with him
the following Saturday to visit his new site. We had to canoe
in, down the Red Deer River.

It had been a dry spring. Paddling down the valley into the
badlands, I could feel the ancient thirst of the land. The
crumbling sides of the valleys with their layers of sediment
appeared more fragile than the yellowed pages of our family
Bible. People and animals had been dying for thousands, mil-
lions of years. John found their remains and tried to make
sense of it all.

I had only one wish: to make sense of my mother's life and
the nagging feeling that I'd let her down.

The site was surrounded by sandy monuments, tall figures
that seemed to be wearing wide, shapeless hats. *Hoodoos,* John
called them. They were silent, accepting their worn-down
fate as my mother had accepted hers. A strong wind whipped
down the valley while John started to dig.

John tried to work, shielding his face with the broad rim
of his hat, but ended up covering the site where he'd started
to dig with a tarp and heavy rocks. Weary, I leaned against one
of the hoodoos, my eyes closed against the wind stirring the
dirt from the ground. I felt myself sinking, about to be buried
under sediment, but John came and took me by the hand.

"Hold on. We'll go in the tent until this wind calms down
again."

I was completely covered by dust, unable to open my eyes. I tried to wipe them, but my hands were every bit as crusty as my face.

"Sit here, Sybil. I'll clean you off with my brushes and then wash your face."

I listened to the wind outside the tent, battering the hoodoos, wearing away the steep sides of the badlands around us. The tent roof flapped and I smelled its musty canvas. I could smell John too, a reassuring, manly smell. Then I felt his fine brush begin its work. He began with my hands, holding them out, gently brushing my fingers, my wrists, then up each arm, across my shoulders, slowly down my chest to my skirt. He dampened a cloth and wiped my face clean. I kept my eyes closed, in a kind of a trance while something welled up inside me.

"What if I'm like some kind of living fossil?" I cried out. "What if you dig down too deep . . . and all you find is the remains of my mother?"

He took my fear seriously, for he answered quietly but earnestly, "Shall I check for you, Sybil?"

Again I felt the little brush on my shoulder, its soft, careful sweeps across my back.

"No. I'm quite certain. It's you, not your mother. You're you, Sybil."

Once I'd started, I couldn't stop. "The life she led used her all up. And she didn't know how to leave it or enjoy it." I thought of her thin, bony back. It had been turned against all of us, not just me. "It's an awful thing not to be able to affect the happiness of someone you love."

With his fingertips, John traced the ridge of my collarbone ever so lightly. "At least you know it's not your fault. And you chose a different life for yourself."

No, it wasn't my fault, nor my father's or my brothers'. It wasn't even my mother's fault. Her fatigue had been a thing beyond her. Outside, the wind was getting quieter, arguing with itself.

"You make *me* happy, Sybil." John's voice was husky. "I don't ever want to miss you like I did this winter. I want to marry you. We can stay here or go back to New York. Anywhere you like."

My eyes flew open and I looked straight into his.

"I don't want to have children. Not for a long time. Probably never!"

He didn't look surprised by my request. "That's fine. We can take precautions. Besides, I like the ones you have right now."

John had a way with observations. I already had twenty children. Eighteen of them boys. And if I was ever going to marry, John was the man for me. He didn't work for the rails, but he wasn't the kind of person who'd shoot a solitary buffalo either. Still, I asked him for a year, knowing I need time to work and think, time to say good-bye to Mama.

When summer holidays came, I took John back to the ranch for a visit. He taught my brothers, even Papa, about fossils, and we spent long afternoons digging up buffalo skulls and arrowheads. But from the very first day, I struck a bargain with them. I'd cook dinner, they'd clean up. Most nights I made our favorite meal the way Mama'd taught me when I was little. Rib roast, browned potatoes with crisp green beans, followed by cinnamon-sweet apple pie. Mama'd been a good cook. After dinner, I left them splashing in the dishwater. I walked for miles along the road, serenaded by crickets and grasshoppers, returning under the first stars to pause beside Mama's grave.

Badlands

In the dark I could smell nasturtiums, imagine their nodding kisses all around me until I turned, eager for the glowing lights of the ranch and the hum and thrum of home.

Sleeping Beauty

JUST BACK FROM SUMMER HOLIDAYS with her da, Lynn looks out the storefront window. A huge flock of chimney swifts is heading for the big smokestack on the hill.

"Help me tally up," Ma says, watching out the window beside her. "Then we'll close for the day." Absently, Ma takes a Pooh-Bah bonbon from one of the big glass jars on the counter and pops it into her mouth. "Strange, them birds . . ." Ma's words are mumble-jumbled. ". . . big flocks every night this week."

Lynn deciphers the slurpy speech, knowing that while she was away fishing with Da on the bay, Ma was eating her way through Mr. Ganong's Fine Confectionery Shop here at home. Years ago, she and Da resigned themselves to Ma's addiction. "Best to say nothing," was Da's solution.

"Please, Ma. Can't I help you later? I haven't seen Cheryl or Moira or Stella."

Sometimes Ma's dependencies get to Lynn. Eight years earlier, when Ma couldn't work anymore in Mr. Ganong's candy factory, the family moved inland to the city to run the little store. But Da missed fishing and the salty air of the coast. The Depression gave Da just the excuse he needed to move back temporarily, just for the season.

"A man's gotta work, gotta put food on the table," Da said when Lynn questioned.

"It's the *real* love of his life," Ma explained later, shrugging wide, tolerant shoulders.

Ma pops a chocolate-centered Chicken Bone. "You'll have plenty of time to catch up with your friends. Speak of the devil," she mumbles, gazing up the street. "Here they come now."

Heronlike, Lynn stretches her long neck to get a better view. "Please, Ma?" she begs. "Tomorrow's the first day of school."

"There's talk of closing schools till October," Ma says, rearranging her mass on the groaning stools beneath her. "Looks like an epidemic. Three cases of polio reported last week. Now Lizzie Fitzgerald, poor soul. All alone and her mister away looking for work."

"What about the twins?" Lynn imagines young Lizzie Fitzgerald as she saw her last—piecing a new quilt, her parlor a meadowy mess of bright cotton flowers. Last spring Lizzie made Lynn her very own quilt—white squares centered with baskets of blue forget-me-nots. In return Lynn took Cecily and John up the hill most evenings. She'd spin out fairy tales for them, especially the twins' favorite, *Sleeping Beauty*. At the top of the hill, they'd sit on a bench to watch the chimney swifts, in front of a sign that read:

The chimney is a communal roosting site for migrating chimney swifts. Without bringing nesting materials into the flue, up to 2,000 of these small birds can enter and

find lodging for the night. On rainless, clear, calm
evenings, they gather and circle in a dark, revolving
doughnut. As dusk approaches, a leader will suddenly
drop into the flue, followed by a precipitous descent of
the whole flock.

"It's a worry all right," Ma says. "Lizzie lying sick, the wee twins roaming the house alone. That quarantine's paralyzed us all. Why, if I could move these feet up the sidewalk, I'd—"

The screen door screeches open. Lynn's three friends step inside, blocking what's left of the evening light. They're dressed in frilly shirtwaists and the shortest skirts Lynn has ever seen.

"Lynn! You're back," Moira says happily, but Stella nudges her in the side and the smile drops from Moira's chubby cheeks.

"We just came in for some candy," Stella says. "Those Chin Chin gums you've been promising us, Mrs. Delcourt." The girls giggle as if they have a private joke. "Think you might find us some, Lynn? Your Ma's been out of them all summer. Must be her favorite this year."

Over the last year, Stella has "forgotten" several times to invite Lynn to a sleepover or a show. Lynn has a sudden vision of Stella as a sinister version of Snow White. Waves of black hair coil around Stella's pale, perfect face, but her features in profile are sharper than the knife Da uses to fillet fish. Perhaps there's a bit of poisoned apple lodged in Stella's heart? Perhaps, one day, she'll wake up *as* the wicked witch.

Stella asks, "Will you be wanting to walk to school with us this year?"

Lynn feels as if she's been slapped across the face. She's

walked to school with Moira, Cheryl, and Stella every morning since she moved here in grade one. Why would high
school be any different?

Stella continues, "Bring a bag of Chin Chins if you do."

Something evil is definitely rising in the caves of Stella's
eyes.

Horrified, Lynn turns to her mother for help but is
shocked by a strange, more disturbing vision. She sees what
she knows Stella sees: an enormous woman, so fat she belongs
in a circus. Lynn shakes her head. No . . . no, it's her ma,
spilling over the two stools beneath her. Confused, Lynn
doesn't know where to look. At the back of the store, the
open door into their kitchen reveals Ma's iron bed, a public
announcement that The Fat Woman can no longer heave
herself upstairs to a bedroom. Ma is an embarrassment, Ma is
a worry. Lynn hops from one feeling to another like a bird
unsure of its footing.

Above Ma's bed is a wedding photo. In 1905—was it really true?—Ma was beautiful, a fine catch, standing beside Da,
the handsome young fisherman in a borrowed suit. She was
the new girl at St. Stephen's, one of Mr. Ganong's girls,
brought over from Scotland to learn the art of hand-dipping
chocolates. Such girls. Such chocolates! The best in the
world! Mr. Ganong himself ate two pounds a day and Ma
brought home bags of them until something snapped in the
soles of her feet. Even standing made her moan with pain,
and Mr. Ganong kindly suggested she run the little shop for
him up in town.

"What a coincidence, you and me with the same taste," Ma
says. "I see a big future for you, Stella. Lynn'll be happy to
bring a bag for you."

Eyes uncertain, Stella purses her red lips. "Come on, girls." She slips her arms around Moira and Cheryl and pulls them toward the screen door. "We don't want to keep the boys waiting."

Lynn ignores her ma and follows her friends outside onto the sidewalk. Usually, Moira or Cheryl would fall back with her, and they'd walk two and two. Not today. Lynn glances at the sky, sees more chimney swifts coming. Doesn't one ever fly off, she wonders? Alone?

Stella stops and sniffs the air. "I smell something fishy. Oh Lynn," she turns around in an exaggerated motion, "is that *you?*"

Whatever lurks in Stella's eyes is fully awake now. Are Moira and Cheryl blind?

Desperate, Lynn asks, "How was your summer, Cheryl?"

"Great. Stella's dad took us to Boston a few weeks ago, shopping. You should have come. We stayed at the Eliot. We ate steak and got new clothes. It was heaven."

It's the first Lynn's heard of the shopping trip. If she'd been invited, she'd gladly have joined them for a little heaven. Like Cheryl, she's made do with hand-me-downs for the last few years. She examines Cheryl's clothes again, carefully. They're so fashionable, they're not even in the 1933 Eaton's catalogue.

"Too bad your dad's down on the coast," Stella says, pausing dramatically. "Must be hard with your parents separated."

Must be hard? Separated? Lynn doesn't think of her family this way. Ma loves the store. Da loves the sea. They spend winters together.

"Your poor father. Must be hard with your mother looking the way she does."

Lynn's cheeks flush bright red. They know nothing about

her parents. How dare they laugh at her mother. Never before has Lynn counted the hours the girls spent playing under the counter while Ma passed candies into their sticky hands—they built worlds for their dolls with Mr. Ganong's empty glass jars in those hours. She counts them now. Thousands? Yes. Thousands of happy hours at her mother's swollen feet.

Lynn feels a hard, sour ball of anger growing inside her. She looks up, needing to spit. Darn those chimney swifts! Such an ugly blot against the sky.

Moira points at Mrs. Fitzgerald's house. "That's the house. They're quarantined. My mother showed us yesterday."

"Let's cross," Cheryl nods. "We can catch it, walking too close."

Rooted to the sidewalk, Lynn watches them run to the other side of the street, clutching each other. "Maybe we could help them?"

"My mother already took them a blueberry pie," Stella argues smugly. Her mother's big tarts win prizes at the church picnic every summer. "Everybody knows Mrs. Fitzgerald had it coming. She didn't keep a clean house."

Up the street, several boys stand waiting. Lynn recognizes the blond head of Stanley Lewis. His dad's the best doctor around, and they live in one of the stately old homes on the finest street in town. Beside him is his best friend, Anthony Duncan. Mr. Duncan runs the funeral parlor and everyone says, "Those two boys'll run the town one day. If Stanley can't cure you, Anthony'll bury you."

Lynn hears their confident voices calling Stella's name, and then appreciative whistles.

Smiling, Stella waves. "Bye, Lynn."

Moira looks over her shoulder. "Coming?"

But Stella's pulling them. "We'll be at the corner. Or the five-and-dime for a soda. You need to change."

Change? Into what?

Something in Mrs. Fitzgerald's bay window attracts Lynn's attention. Two small faces are stuck to the glass, the pale faces of Cecily and John. Cecily's sucking her thumb, which she's not allowed to do. Lynn waves. Their faces disappear and the curtain flutters briefly.

The white shutters on either side of Mrs. Fitzgerald's bay window reflect the feverish pink of sunset. Below them, the green grass has grown long and patchy, crying out for a trim.

Lynn backs away, toward her own house.

"Ma," she shouts anxiously from the doorway.

"I'm still here, pet," Ma says. She hasn't budged off the stools. "No need to yell." She's closing the lids on the jars.

"When will Mr. Fitzgerald be home?"

"Is that what's bothering you? Tomorrow," Ma sighs. "They've contacted him, thank God."

"The twins might be hungry—"

"The church women are taking food over." Ma closes the blind on the window and mutters, "I need to soak my feet. Tomorrow, I'll get myself up to Lizzie's."

The store is officially closed for the day.

Lynn watches her mother balance and grope her way through the shadows to the back kitchen.

"Oh, my aching feet. Lynn dear, turn the radio on for me. Must be time for *Amos and Andy.*"

Lynn settles her Ma, then rushes back into the store, where she closes all the blinds. The faces of Cecily and John haunt her, their small foreheads blobbed against the bay window.

Where's Lizzie Fitzgerald? Is she lying paralyzed on the parlor sofa, surrounded by cotton flowers? Or upstairs in her bed, listening to worrisome noises she can't check?

Ma can barely get herself into the kitchen. There's no way she'll get up the street to help them. Impulsively, Lynn dumps chocolates into a paper bag, grabs a bottle of milk from the icebox, and runs outside. The backs of her muscled, bare legs match the feverish pink of the shutters on either side of the Fitzgeralds' bay window.

She glances furtively toward the corner where the boys are still clustered around Moira and Cheryl, Stella dead center.

What if they look her way? She winces at the thought of being caught. What will her future hold then? Stella will pass notes at school. Backs will turn. There'll be hushed whispers as she walks by. It won't matter how many Chin Chins she brings, her friends won't walk to school with her.

Friends? They're Stella's followers. Why, they're as brainless as chimney swifts! Lynn runs onto the verandah of the Fitzgeralds' house.

Strange—there's a train of cardboard boxes leading to the door. Lynn steps carefully around them, spying loaves of bread going stale, questionable casseroles, and bundles wrapped in red, checkered cloths. The scent of blueberries makes her nauseous.

The twins turned three last winter. On tippy-toes, they're not tall enough to grasp the front doorknob and yank it open. Lynn puts an ear to the door. Silence. How long would it take the twins to starve to death inside? What if they're sick with polio? Cripes, what is she doing? She should leave the milk and chocolates out here and be done with it.

She glances nervously behind her. Above the smokestack, the chimney swifts sweep dark shadowy circles across the sky.

Lynn turns the dull brass knob and shoves open the door. It swings quietly on its hinges, thuds to a stop as it hits a wall.

Staring at her, seated on the bottom steps of the oak stairway, are the twins. They're in their pajamas. Lynn avoids looking left into the front parlor with its bay window and sofa.

She almost says *I see you're ready for bed,* but thinks the better of it. Their pajamas are rumpled and dirty and the house has a new, unpleasant odor, the stench of dried-up pee.

Cecily pulls her thumb from her mouth. "Where's my da?"

Lynn's mouth goes dry. She struggles to swallow and find some answers. "He's coming. You'll see him soon. Tomorrow. You hungry?"

Cecily nods.

Lynn opens the bottle of milk, passes it to Cecily, gives the bag to John. "Chocolates. You should share them. Give some to your mother."

John's eyes go big and round. "She's theeping," he says.

Theeping? Lynn's mind snags on the word.

"She won't wake up." He shakes his head, bewildered.

Lynn remembers his lisp. She gives him a quick hug though she knows she shouldn't. *Quarantine.* How can she not touch him when his mother is inside somewhere and won't wake up?

She shoves her hands in her pockets, rocks back and forth, presses her lips, and suddenly thinks of a new version of their favorite fairy tale. "Maybe it's like an enchantment. Somebody cast an evil spell and she can't wake up until tomorrow. Your ma'll wake up when your da comes home and kisses her."

Both twins brighten with the same dimpled smile.

"Like Theeping Beauty," John says.

Lynn feels the unwanted pressure of tears behind her eyes. "I gotta go. But you come get me if . . ." Abruptly, she turns, leaving the door ajar in case . . . she hates to think much further . . . in case there are witches in the night.

On the verandah, she steps carefully around the derailed boxes until she finds the one she wants. Her left foot squishes, leaving a deep, blue print in the prize-winning crust.

The street is empty. The sun has finally crawled beneath the dark blanket of night. Above the open mouth of the smokestack, a first chimney swift dives inside, straight down, disappearing from sight. Immediately, another one follows, and then, as if tied to each other, the whole flock spirals downward, draining the sky, into the hungry hole.

No Missing Parts

ONE JUNE EVENING in 1943, an evening when the light lingered and I was allowed to stay out late, my older brother Jim didn't come home.

I was sitting with Gertie, our knobby knees jutting out like crows' tails on the fence my father had built between our backyards.

"I'm hungry. Got anything?"

"Nothing, Ruthie. Can't you go in and get a snack?"

"I don't dare. Mom's in a mood, watching for Jim. He's usually home at five-thirty, right after work."

We heard a clatter of metal pots from inside my house.

"Bet he's out with Denise," Gertie said. "I saw them kissing, Sunday after church. They thought they were hidden by the big oaks in the cemetery, near where your dad is. Jim had his hands right here."

Gertie and I were eagerly awaiting what our mothers called "development." Gertie covered her tiny breasts with her hands and promptly fell off the fence.

I laughed at her. "Well, Jim's not the only one. While he was busy working last Saturday with Uncle Matt, she was busy in an alley off Main Street letting Ted Bumstead do the same thing. *More,* Gertie." I gave her a meaningful look before I continued. "I should warn Jim. Uncle Matt says she's just a hummingbird after nectar. Sucks one dry, then flits on to the next."

At that moment, my mother called, "Ruth! Set the table!" The back screen door slammed. I jumped off the fence and ran.

"Meet me here after dinner," I called back.

Inside, I could hear the boarders upstairs, washing up. Mom had taken in boarders after Dad died, two well-paying boarders. Most days, as soon as they were in the front door, Mom watched out the window that gave her a clear view up Pine Street. "Jim's coming!" she'd sing out when she spied him at the top of the hill.

I set five places as usual. "Think Jim's with Denise?"

"That's none of our business, missy. Don't forget the butter knife."

Jim's empty place brought an uneasy silence to the table. Mother's fingertips drummed beside her plate, her eyes intently turned to the window and the view up the street. After supper she refused my help with the dishes, said she needed something to occupy her mind. I grabbed fresh macaroons to share with Gertie and slipped out. Perched on the fence again, we chewed warm coconut and breathed in the heady scent of lilacs.

Gertie wiped her fingers on her shirt and began plaiting my frizzy red hair into a smooth braid. "Here's what I think," she continued, right where she'd left off. "With those huge eyes and that black hair, maybe Denise bewitches men."

"Not Jim. He's too levelheaded. For seven years, he's been the man of our family taking care of us."

I remembered back to when I was six, just after Dad died. Jim had persuaded Mom to take us into Toronto, said I needed to see the Santa Claus parade. He'd carried me for hours on his shoulders while Mom scolded, "Put her down, Jim. No sense spoiling her."

But he wouldn't. "She'll be the first to see Santa," he'd laughed. Jim would have lifted me to the moon if I'd asked.

Gertie lowered her voice like the women did when they were about to share some particularly un-Christian gossip. "Mrs. Franklin told my mother that Denise was wearing Kevin Stewart's ring before he left for the war."

"Before Kevin lost his legs. That's what she means, Gertie."

"Must be awful to lose your legs, then your girl too. Kevin Stewart doesn't go anywhere except the Stewarts' front porch. When you walk by their place at night, all you see is the spooky red glow of his cigarette in a dark corner. Something must be wrong with the boys in Woodstock, going after a girl who's all looks and no heart."

I stood up on the railings, ready to defend my brother. "Jim just hasn't seen through Denise yet. He blames Kevin. Says he turned bitter and drove her away."

"Love sure is blind in Woodstock."

But I knew it wasn't love. It was the war. The war was like a skunk living under the house. There was nowhere to escape. The odor had even reached upstairs, into our cupboards, into our dreams.

Gertie must have read my thoughts because she suddenly asked, "Do you think Jim'll go?"

That was the fear that woke me up some nights. "Jim gets real quiet when we listen to the news on the radio," I said.

The evening grew dark and quiet around us. Gertie and I

watched the sky slowly burn away, embers of a distant sun, imagining all the men, all the boys we knew fighting under an exploding sky, halfway across the earth. I found the North Star and pointed it out to Gertie.

A door slammed not far away. The kitchen light in my house went on, throwing its white lifeline across the backyards.

"Kept your dinner warm." My mother's voice drifted across the lawn.

"Jim's home!" I sprang from the fence.

Gertie called as I ran toward the light. "Tell me everything tomorrow. Call on me early."

The screen door squeaked when I yanked it open. I stood there, hypnotized by the sight of Jim. He was ambling across the kitchen, throwing me his cheerful salute before he sat down at his place at the end of our table, the place reserved for Jim.

My mother fumbled with her oven mitts, pushing off the tin plate that insulated his dinner. Jim's dark hair was smoothed back, a good imitation of Cary Grant. He leaned forward into the steam, breathing deeply. One stubborn curl escaped down his forehead. "Ahh," he sighed, closing his eyes. "You make the world's best meatballs, Ma."

"Utter nonsense," she said, but she couldn't help laughing, couldn't resist pulling one hand from a mitt and smoothing back that curl.

"We didn't eat dinner till eight waiting for you." I glared at him. If Mom wasn't going to get mad at him, I sure was. "Where've you been?"

Jim leaned back in his chair and gave me an eerie smile. "Fraser Hamilton got his dad's truck. We went into Toronto. To Manning Depot."

My hand slipped off the door and it slammed shut. Manning Depot was where the men enlisted. "I thought . . . I thought you had a date."

Jim laughed. "A date with the RCAF. Ma understands. I hope you will too, Ruthie. I can't stay any longer, not while they're fighting. I'm going to be a pilot, kiddo."

He picked up his knife and swooped it through the air, gliding and diving over enemy mashed potatoes and islands of meatballs.

I stopped him, grabbing his wrist. "You've got some kind of exemption. We need you here."

"Ruthie, let him go." My mother wrapped one arm firmly around my shoulders, pulling me away from him. "This is up to Jim."

She pushed me toward the hallway and the stairs. "Go on now, up to bed. Things will look different in the morning. We'll make out fine."

How could she possibly say *make out fine?* I held on to the newel. "When do you—"

Mother poked me in the ribs.

"Three weeks," he answered, landing his bomber beside his plate.

Twenty days later, Jim left for training. But not before he took out all his savings to buy Denise Madison a ring. Their engagement was announced at Holy Trinity Anglican Church. The minister asked, "Does anyone here have just cause why these two should not be married?"

I jumped up in our pew. My mother pulled me down before I could scream out, "Yes! She's a witch!"

At home, Jim leaped up the stairs two, sometimes three, at a time. I feared he would take off and fly right out the window, cheating me of our last days together. One day he gave me money to buy my first lipstick at the five-and-dime, warning me to hide it from Mom, and the next day, he was gone.

IN THOSE FIRST MONTHS following Jim's departure, if my mother left the door to Jim's room open after dusting it, I'd slip in there. His leather high school jacket hung on the back of his door; the sweat from his armpits had stained the lining inside the sleeves with dark circles. I could smell him. *Jim*. His image came back to me clearly then, me sitting on his broad shoulders, high above the crowd, watching for Santa.

I held his coat and was glad he hadn't given it to Denise.

But then a strange day came, after he'd finished training and gone overseas, when his image wouldn't come to me. I felt alone, bereft of his presence. So I took his coat. I slipped it off the hook, saying the little prayer I always said: "Just send him back, Lord. We don't care about missing parts." I packed his coat carefully in an old Eaton's box and hid it under some sweaters at the top of my closet.

BY THIS TIME IN THE WAR, we knew what it meant when a stranger in uniform delivered a telegram. He'd square his shoulders before knocking on the front door. The mother in the house would be in the kitchen, doing up the last of the dishes, drying her hands on her apron. She didn't watch out the window anymore. She hadn't noticed the stranger approach. Wasn't it odd how dry her mouth felt? And how hushed everything had become! There was only the tap, tap, tap as her feet crossed her polished hardwood floor to answer the front door in the middle of the afternoon. There he stood, the dreaded messenger, the one we had wished upon our neighbor and then asked for God's forgiveness. He waited while she read, shifting his feet. He knew what it said. Her son was shot down in action. There would be a gravestone for him somewhere in Brittany. He was sorry.

I was sitting with Gertie on the verandah when the stranger in uniform walked down Pine Street. I watched him stop and check the number of our house. Gertie grabbed my hand when he turned up my walkway, up my front steps.

"This the Donahue residence?" he asked.

My heart was knocking like a wild, desperate thing in my chest. I warned myself: *If you don't answer him, don't even look, he'll have to take it somewhere else.* Gertie stared at me, then pressed her other hand against her mouth.

"Is your mother home?"

Don't look! Don't look! But Gertie did. She nodded, and he went to the door.

We turned and watched him at the doorway, shifting his feet before he left.

A car passed. The dust flew up and then settled back over the little stones covering the road, waiting for the next passing car.

"Oh, Ruthie," Gertie whispered, before she ran home. "You'd best go in."

I wanted somewhere to run too. But I was already home.

IN A SMALL TOWN, bad news spreads as quick as warm honey. Yet it took Denise Madison over a month to come by and pay her respects. I was sitting with Gertie on our verandah, watching clouds and a pale moon, saying nothing, feeling nothing, just watching those clouds drift past that queer, pale moon in an afternoon sky.

A cream-colored Buick drove by and then backed up like an afterthought. Next thing we knew, we were watching Denise Madison's long legs poke out of Ted Bumstead's car. She didn't bother to look at us.

Her respects to my mother were the quick kind. Ted Bumstead kept the car running. She was back out of our house in the time it takes to swat a fly, but just as she got to the top step, one of her heels stuck in a little hole between the floorboards.

That's when I stopped watching. I sprang onto the second step, smack-dab in front of her. "Jim's ring," I demanded, holding out my hand.

"Why, little Ruthie . . ." She yanked her shoe one last time before giving up. "I didn't see you there."

"You're not leaving with my brother's ring."

I pointed up to the sky, to the ghostly reflection hovering above us. "See that?" I hissed. "Jim's up there watching you. He sees right through you now. If you don't give me that ring—I know Jim—he'll be coming after you for it himself."

That's when I grabbed her hand, while she was staring dumbstruck at the moon. I twisted the ring hard over her knuckle.

"Now, get off our property!" I hollered at the top of my lungs.

Teetering on one high heel, Denise fled to the car, her black hair streaming behind her. She flung herself into the Buick, just as I wrenched her shoe out of the hole in our verandah. I ran down the steps and pitched it after her. It ricocheted off the back fender and into the cloud of dust that was swirling up Pine Street.

Every muscle in me began to shake, out of control. I

turned around. My mother and Gertie were standing together on the top step, holding each other, staring at me like I was a stranger possessed with demons.

"I'm not giving it back!" I shouted defiantly. "Jim shouldn't have given it to her. And he never should have gone."

A look came over my mother's face. She pulled herself up tall and said, "Those were Jim's choices. We're going to respect that." She spoke in the quiet, soothing voice she used whenever I was sick. "But if Denise didn't want that ring bad enough . . . it's yours. You keep it."

"Why'd he ever pick that pea-brained, two-timing Denise?"

My mother winced. "He was only nineteen, Ruthie. He didn't have enough time."

The diamond was burning a hole in my palm. I uncurled my fingers and looked at it. I stared into its faces, the sunlight trapped inside, sizzling, forcing me to shut my eyes.

And then strangely, for the first time in months, Jim's image, his broad handsome face, came back to me. I started to spin. Slowly at first. Then faster, remembering when I was little, Jim holding me firmly by the wrists, my feet leaving the cool, green grass, spinning faster and faster, until finally . . . I let go and hurled Jim's ring toward the sky, toward the shrouded moon.

Author's Note

"No Missing Parts" was inspired by my mother's stories about the war years. She actually had four older brothers who fought in World War II. She was closest to the youngest of those brothers, Jim. He was the only one not to come back. Fifty years later, in 1994, she found and visited his grave in Brittany, France.

Inexplicable things happen when you write. Sometime after this story was first published, my mother took me aside one evening.

"Who told you Jim was engaged to a girl like Denise?" she asked me with a strange look.

My mother is a quiet, proud woman who once told me a story about a "friend of one of her brothers" who got engaged to a two-timing girl. But as happens in storytelling, this became part of my fictionalized Uncle Jim.

"No one," I answered. "I made it up."

"It happened to Jim," she said, "much like you told it. Except for one thing. He came back on a leave. Only once, and he found out about Denise."

"That must have been awful for him."

She took my hand and led me to her room, to her mahogany dresser. She opened a little drawer at the top, in the middle, and took out a tiny, dark blue jewelry box.

I felt the moon come into the room, a little closer.

"He made Denise give him back the ring. Jim gave it to me. All these years, I've been the keeper of my brother's ring, wondering what to do with it."

She opened the box. Inside was a delicate diamond ring.

"When I read your story, I knew I should give it to you. I think you're its keeper now."

Leaving the Iron Lung

"It's hockey night in Canada. In goal for the Montreal Canadiens . . . Gump Worsley," I holler in my best imitation of Foster Hewitt.

This gets the desired reaction from the kitchen. "Quiet, Pauline! I'm on the phone, long distance with Grand-mère."

"In goal for the Toronto Maple Leafs . . . Johnny Bower!" This time I whistle, long and shrill. Grand-mère knows the only thing I enjoy more than hockey is getting my mother good and mad.

My mother's heels click across the kitchen floor. I wait with my shriveled legs to one side of my favorite place, the cushioned window seat overlooking our backyard. When I was little, I used to wait at the kitchen window for my mother's lessons, watching other kids on their way to school, until one day a girl stopped and pointed at me.

"Look!" the girl yelled. "That's Polio Pauline! My mother says she got it from the Don Mills pool." Four girls stared at me, horrified. I stuck out my tongue, and they ran, afraid they might catch it.

I position the players of my father's old table-hockey set

for a face-off. Here on my cotton-chintz rink, the blue, paint-chipped Leafs never lose.

"Pauline!"

My mother sweeps the metal men into the cigar box where I store them. Before I can grab the pleats of her gray flannel skirt, she shoves the box on top of a bookcase.

My canes are out of reach. "Not fair!" I yell.

"You did that to annoy me. Why aren't you reading?"

I turn away from her. Out the window, I see my father skating smooth figure eights around our huge backyard rink, and I wish for the thousandth time: if only I could fly like that, powerful and free.

"This might be Grand-mère's last Christmas." My mother's voice is softer now, conciliatory, but her hands fuss nervously with the perfect bun of her hair. "She wants to come and see us."

"Can't one of your sisters bring her?"

"They're too busy. They have families of their own."

"Tante Marie doesn't. You could ask Tante Marie."

"You know how hard I find her visits. She interferes. Stirs up trouble. She even flirts with your father."

Tante Marie is my mother's youngest sister, twelve years younger. Where my mother is hard bones, smelling like a closed-up library, Tante Marie is soft curves and whiffs of lavender and the open woods. Her dark hair is never pinned back but swings playfully around her shoulders. She makes my father and me laugh—is that what flirting is? Something always happens when she visits, some wonderful trouble.

TWO WEEKS REMAIN until Christmas, Christmas of 1963. It only takes me two days to wear my mother down—I simply refuse to read any of the books she brings me until she invites Tante Marie. Four aunts and Grand-mère call me a self-centered, twelve-year-old cripple, thinking I don't understand when they whisper *gâtée* in French. But I'll do anything to see Tante Marie. She never speaks a word against me, not in any language.

As USUAL, the moment Tante Marie steps inside our front door, my mother turns into the ice queen.

"Ma belle." Tante Marie gathers me close, kissing both my cheeks. Her skin feels warm and electric. Even her perfume embraces me. "You've grown so tall. Come, get your coat and we'll walk."

My mother protests, "Outside? It's too icy. She could fall."

"Ridicule!" Tante Marie tousles my perfectly bobbed hair. "She can't stay in all day."

"What do you know about it, Marie?"

"Mes filles," scolds Grand-mère, shaking a bony finger at them.

"She needs to walk every day, get outdoors. Books aren't enough, Agathe."

"Polio crippled her legs, not her mind."

"Agatha!" My father speaks sharply from the living room, where he is seating Grand-mère. "Let them go for a walk."

"Pauline doesn't like to walk. Ask her yourself."

I hate when they do this. "Yes! I'll walk with Tante Marie." I do up my coat and shuffle out the doorway.

"We'll be back in time for drinks," Tante Marie laughs over her shoulder. "We'll run the whole way back."

Outside, I lurch slowly down Chelsea Street. I keep my head down in case someone is gawking at me from a window. My father calls Don Mills the postwar dream for happy families. Everything along these wide streets, from the big backyards to the central library, has been carefully planned. Everything but the outbreak of polio when I was two.

"You know, Tante Marie," I stop to catch my breath, seeking a dry patch of asphalt so my canes won't slip, "I can't run."

"How do you know that? Me, I dream one day my art, it will be in the Louvre." I follow Tante Marie's gesture as she points dramatically toward the east, toward Paris. "Everybody's got a dream. You too, *n'est-ce pas, chérie?*"

I've never admitted my dream to anyone. Now's my chance, with Tante Marie beside me, pointing beyond the horizon. Her cheeks are so brilliant, they almost match the blazing red of her beret. No one wears a red beret in Don Mills.

"One day . . . I want to skate with my father," I say, biting my lip.

"Ahh. That's a wonderful dream. Before I go back to *Montréal,* I'm gonna do something about that."

Tante Marie is the only adult I know who keeps her promises. On Christmas Eve, after all the gifts are handed out, she pulls out two hockey sticks from behind the tree, each tied with a red velvet ribbon. One she hands to my father, the other, winking, to me.

My mother sits at the far end of our blue and red braided rug, unwrapping her last gift. "What?" she asks faintly. "What will Pauline do with a hockey stick?"

Tante Marie laughs as if my mother has told a funny joke. "She'll play hockey! Will can push her on the rink in her wheelchair."

"On the ice? That's crazy. . . ."

But my father spins Marie around and kisses her, right on

the lips. Grand-mère tisks and looks away. "There's nothing I'd like better than to play hockey with Pauline," he says. "Why didn't I think of it before?"

Tante Marie ties the red velvet ribbons together and places them, a *couronne* in Grand-mère's white curls. Tisking again, Grand-mère turns away, only to catch sight of her image in the large mirror over the sofa. Unexpectedly, her face unwraps with laughter.

A month later, Tante Marie phones to tell us Grand-mère died in her sleep. My parents argue all evening about who will go to the funeral. I fall asleep, dreaming that Grand-mère lies in a round coffin, round like the iron lung that once forced me to breathe. Her head, adorned with red ribbons, sticks out from one end. She scowls at us in a little mirror above her head, angled to let her see the reflection of people behind her. In the morning, I wake up to find my mother has taken the early train, alone, to Montreal.

I fear I will never get to see Tante Marie again. Only her gift remains, hidden in the garage. While it feels like my mother has slammed the door on seeing Tante Marie, I realize that another door has opened.

"Let's play hockey," I say.

My father doesn't think twice about it. "Good idea." He smiles and the mood between us brightens. When we're ready he carries me outside to my wheelchair, tucking my legs beneath several blankets.

He hands me my stick, then skates behind me slowly. "Faster!" I yell and he picks up speed. "Faster!" We start to soar around the rink. My job is to raise the puck as we approach the net full-speed, seeking the sweet target of a corner pocket.

"She shoots, she scores!" he yells and I smack Tante Marie's gift triumphantly against the ice. He only dumps me once. We hit a bump and I fly right out of the chair, my leg braces scraping across the ice until I tangle to a stop in the bottom of the net.

I sit up slowly. "I'm not hurt," I reassure him.

"She shoots, she scores!" my father yells again. We look furtively toward the house. The window is empty and we start to laugh, hysterical puffs of laughter that sail into the Don Mills sky while our tears freeze, salty crystals on our reddened cheeks.

THE FOLLOWING YEAR, winter comes early to Don Mills, right after Halloween. My father and I decide to lay out the boards and do the first spraying of water for our rink. But before we can go out, Mother stops us. "Have you told her yet?"

"No. I thought you should."

"What is it? Did someone die?"

"No," my father laughs at me. "The opposite. Your mother is going to—"

I gasp, noticing for the first time the round bulge of her usually flat belly. "How could you? You're too old!"

"I am not!"

"We don't need a baby."

"We're having one."

"Maybe it'll get polio."

She gasps. "Pauline . . . how can you say that? That's cruel."

I shove my touque down over my ears. I don't want a sister or brother who can run and skate.

My father puts an arm around me, but I shrug him off and

glare at the black and white linoleum. "There's a vaccine now," he says. "It won't happen again. This baby will be a blessing for all of us."

"When's this *blessing* coming?"

"The baby's due in March. Your father will come to the hospital with me. Someone will have to stay with you." She hesitates. "I've asked my sisters."

I look up quickly. My throat aches. "Did you ask Tante Marie?"

"You'd like that, wouldn't you?" But she's not speaking to me. She's looking at my father while her hand skates uneasy circles around her belly.

ALL THAT WINTER, the weather stays cold, right into March, right until the day of Tante Marie's arrival. With the approach of the train from Quebec, the mercury fires up the thermometer outside our back window and my mother goes into instant labor. By the time my father brings Marie home from Union Station, gloomy pools of water threaten our rink and my mother's contractions are coming regularly.

I listen to the commotion in the front hall as my father fetches my mother's hospital bag. They kiss me hurriedly and leave.

At long last, I am alone with Tante Marie.

She drags an enormous bag beside my window seat. Like a magician, she pulls out smocked dresses and knitted sets of baby booties and sweaters. I laugh with delight when I spy, at the bottom, a brand new table-hockey game.

"Your *maman* will wonder at me, not bringing you a book or a dress."

I twirl the rod closest to me. One of the players does a perfect pirouette in the center of the rink. "I hate dresses. They only show my legs."

"Let's play then. I'm gonna be *les Canadiens.*" She winks and I know that my very own blessing has arrived. Kneeling at the other end of my window seat, Tante Marie smokes and curses all week as we abandon ourselves to a Stanley Cup final. Tante Marie is a fanatical opponent! A worthy opponent.

Somewhere in a hospital in downtown Toronto, my mother gives birth to a baby girl. The evening my parents and new sister are expected back home, I bring out my old cigar box.

"Maybe you'll stay a few more weeks?" I beg.

"Maybe. Let's play our last game with these guys."

"The only time we're happy is when you're here."

"We? Are you speaking for your *maman* too?"

"She's never happy," I say bitterly, dumping out the metal men. "Are you sure you're really sisters? How did she ever leave Quebec in the first place?"

"What's wrong with you tonight?"

"Talk to me! No one tells me anything around here."

"What do you want to know, *chérie?* About your *maman?"* She sighs. "I remember Agathe always with a book. She loved English literature more than anything in the world. She was so thrilled when she won a scholarship to study here. Then she met your papa and made Toronto her home."

"But why does she have to be so ...so ..."

"Pauline," she says quietly, gently. "The summer you became very sick with polio, your *maman* had to take you to the hospital. At the time, she was almost a professor at the *université.* She was French. She was a woman. You can't imagine how hard she'd worked to get there."

"I spoiled her life, you mean."

"No!" she shakes her head emphatically. "Nothing could be worse than watching them strap you, a sick, helpless child, inside that horrible iron lung." She shudders as she remembers, pausing before she can continue. "It seemed like such a miracle when you finally got better and they let you come home. Right or wrong, Agathe gave up her life at the university because she wanted to protect you."

It's my turn to shudder. I try to imagine how we might be, if she'd stayed at the university, if she'd let me go to school. "But it's like she crippled both of us," I whisper.

Tante Marie nods sadly, picks up Gump, and twists him absently between her fingers.

There's still another question burning inside me. Do I dare ask it? I take Gump from her and stand him in goal. "Were you in love with my father?"

"Phew . . . you're too much tonight!"

"Were you?"

"Agathe is my sister. Your papa is her husband. That's *that.*"

"Then why is she so jealous? Why can't you get along, like real sisters?"

Tante Marie looks out the window. The temperature is dropping rapidly and the pools of water on the backyard rink are shrinking as they freeze. "Grand-mère once told me," she answers bitterly, "Agathe hated me the moment I was born."

She reaches out and squeezes my hand hard. "It's too late. Let's play. I'm going to beat Toronto so bad . . ."

We throw ourselves into the game. In the last period, Tante Marie knocks over one of my Leafs. I make a buzzer sound and give her a penalty. For three minutes, she has to play sitting on one hand. Somehow she manages to score immediately from the face-off and this seems hilarious to both of us.

"With one hand! I beat Toronto with one hand!"

She scoops me up and swings me around, my legs flapping wildly. *"Maudits Anglais!* Those damn Englishmen!" We laugh and scream.

"Arrêt! Enough, Marie." The brittle voice of my mother stops us.

My parents stand in the doorway, staring at us, their mouths open wide. A chill enters the room, a glacier sliding over us, unstoppable. My feet slide awkwardly to the floor. If only we'd heard them come in!

My mother speaks again. "I should've known better than to trust you, Marie. Do you forget this is my home? Put her down."

"Agatha, they're just having fun," my father pleads.

Everything about my mother seems to be cracking, her face, her voice, her hands. Shocked, we watch her thrust a small bundle, which I realize must be my sister, toward my father. In a shattered voice, she says to him, "You always take Marie's side. But I know how she tries to divide us, to cause trouble. I want her to leave."

She turns abruptly and runs up the stairs. We hear the click of her door. She might as well have slammed it.

A strange feeling comes over me, as if I'm looking into one of those curved mirrors at a circus where we become skinny giants, fat midgets, and unrecognizable families.

"She's exhausted," my father says wearily. "I suppose we should all get to bed. Do you want to hold your new sister?" he asks me.

I make my buzzer sound and stare out the window. "Temperature's fallen, Dad. Let's go check the ice."

"It's too late, Pauline," he says, shaking his head. "Maybe tomorrow . . . and maybe tomorrow you'll be happy to hold her."

"I never asked for a sister. Why should I?"

"Because I need you to. . . ." There is an edge to his voice. "Did you ever think of that?" He switches off the light and turns away, disappearing up the stairs too.

Johnny Bower lies flat on his face across the goal crease. I hurl him across the room.

Tante Marie grabs my wrist and whispers harshly, "Don't be this way, Pauline!" The anger in her voice scares me.

The house is so suddenly quiet, I hear the furnace click on in the basement, then a rush of air up the vents as if the house is beginning to breathe. For a terrifying moment, I feel as if I'm back in the iron lung. I remember vividly how it closed around me, forcing out my breath . . . always pressing.

I want to cry like a baby, but, looking into Tante Marie's fierce eyes, I see the hurt caused by my mother. I gulp a huge, deep breath . . . and nod.

"I do want to hold her," I admit, regretting how carelessly I spoke to my father. "Besides. That's a big rink out there and we could use a goalie."

"Good." She laughs and wipes any trace of hurt from her eyes, passing me my canes.

"I'll leave in the morning, Pauline. It's best. In the future, whenever you want to visit me, I'll send you a train ticket. I won't come here again. You're almost fourteen, old enough to come to *Montréal* by yourself."

I start to tremble at the thought of traveling alone on the train.

"Yes, you can do it. Besides," she says with a wink, "I want to show you *Montréal,* take you to the Forum. That's where we'll really beat those *maudits Anglais."*

Oh, she makes me laugh! I breathe in the familiar scent of lavender as I stand beside her, no longer trembling on my canes. Moonlight casts a long, six-legged shadow of us toward the front door, while behind us, one last mirror of water remains on the backyard rink. I see our reflection out there, briefly, before the picture vanishes, turning opaque as ice.

Saying Good-Bye
to Princess Di

DIANA PRACTICES "the look" in a floor-to-ceiling mirror from Home Depot: chin down, eyes mascaraed wide like a deer caught in the high beams.

With her short, streaked hair, she looks remarkably like her namesake, the Princess of Wales. This summer, however, since turning sixteen, if Diana stares too long in the mirror she gets an irresistible urge to make faces. She spikes up her hair and stares long and hard at her navel where she dreams of getting a piercing. If she had the nerve she'd get a hoop ring with a bead.

She tries talking to her mother, but it's impossible. Mom's too caught up in this particular fantasy. "You're special. When you were little, the princess waved at *you.*"

"Oh, Mom," Diana groans, "she waves at everybody on TV."

"You were born on July 29th, 1981. The very same day as the royal wedding. *The very same day!* Don't you see what that means? You live under the same lucky star. Goodness, you were even born in a city named after her great-great-grand-mother."

"Victoria doesn't count, Mom. We've lived in North Vancouver most of my life. Besides, maybe I want to be different, choose my own destiny. What if I dyed my hair green?"

"Cool," says her little brother, Matthew. He jumps down from the top of the entertainment unit. "Can I help?"

"Don't you dare," says Diana's boyfriend, Ken. He calls Matthew "monkey brother," tells him to shut up. Ken's hot. He has bleached hair, a pretty-boy face, and a hunk of a body. The girls at school eye Diana with looks that say, *Put on twenty pounds, break out in zits, let me have him.*

August heats up. So do their arguments. Ken says, "Why would you want to look freaky? I know a hundred girls who'd die to look like Di. You're lucky you're thin. You don't even have to throw up."

Fat lot you know. I haven't had chocolate for months, Diana thinks. At night she dreams of truffles and Sweet Marie bars, Kit Kats and—

Matthew interrupts. He hates Ken. "You're sick. You make *me* want to throw up."

"We're heading for the rhubarb," Mom says. She drags Matthew outside. Mom works in a beauty salon. She prefers life pretty and polished. She'll do anything to avoid a sour scene.

Diana's undecided about staying out of the rhubarb patch. Sure, at first she liked being the envy of every girl at school, but lately, being with Ken makes her feel . . . insecure.

AT THE VERY END OF AUGUST, Princess Di's lucky star explodes. Bits of star molecules scatter throughout the universe. One lands in Diana's bathroom where she's got the radio on beside a hot plate and a pot of wax. She's doing her eyebrows when she hears the news: *Diana, Princess of Wales, is dead.*

She gasps. Burns herself. She can't believe it. She cringes from the pain in her eyebrows, from the shock of the news, unable to take it in. Princess Di was in a car accident last night . . . was rushed to a hospital . . . *and is dead?*

Beside the sink are magazines with Di's photo on the cover. "No!" she cries and picks one up, shows it to the mirror. "It's not possible. She's alive. It couldn't happen to Di. She's too beautiful. Look!"

Fingers shaking, she changes the station. It can't be true. It's got to be some kind of sick joke. Who's that guy they talked about at school? Orson Welles with an end-of-the-world radio play? But no, it's no joke. It's the same news on the next station and the next. Princess Di was in a car accident and now she's dead.

All that day, and the next, Diana feels numb. She's in shock. She can't eat a thing. All week she picks at her meals in front of the TV. She doesn't dream of chocolate but of car chases, cameras, and flashing lights. When she's not watching TV, she pores over old magazines, staring at Di's pictures. The Royal Wedding . . . some fairy-tale ending *that* turned out to be. Total bummer. The prince fell in love with another woman. Why did Princess Di get such a lousy beginning and then this, this awful ending?

Diana stares at the glossy photo of her high school prom last June. She and Ken were voted The Royal Couple. Diana's doubts go wild. What if she had serious problems—worse than zits or twenty pounds? Like, what if she were in a disfiguring accident? She rolls her eyeballs backward and sucks in her cheeks. Would Ken love her if she looked like the living dead?

Friday night, she says to Ken, "I've set my alarm so I can watch the live coverage of the funeral in England."

"That's dumb. They're calling for clear skies tomorrow. If you're up all night, you'll be a zombie. You always said Princess Di wasn't a selfish person, and here you are only thinking about yourself, letting this wreck the last perfect weekend of the summer."

Every weekend, if it's not raining, Ken picks her up in his dad's BMW. Usually, they go to Kitsilano Beach for a work-out. According to Ken, "That's where the chicks are at. You know how an audience keeps us on our toes."

Saturday morning Diana wakes up to sunshine pouring through the window and Ken pounding at the door. *Damn.* How did this happen? Crying, she runs to turn on the TV in the front room and lets Ken in.

"I missed it," she sobs. "My alarm didn't go off."

"What do you mean—missed it? Think about it. It's not like you were actually going to be at the funeral. So what if you watch it another time?"

Although it's not Ken's intention, there's a ray of consolation in what he's saying. She wipes her eyes and turns to the TV, listening to the commentators. Ken's right. They're going to replay the funeral all day, starting with the procession through London. She bites her lip. Ken puts his arm around her shoulder. She sinks into him.

"Now go make yourself gorgeous."

Not knowing why she feels suddenly disappointed, Diana heads to the bathroom, where she gets dressed in record time, not caring what she wears. She hears the drone of the TV commentators and the angry blip of an exchange between Ken and Matthew. It takes several attempts to get makeup on. She keeps crying and her face is a mess.

The drone stops suddenly. Ken's shut off the TV.

Diana runs to the living room. "Aren't we going to watch the funeral? Can't we go to the beach later?"

Ken blocks the screen. Calmly, firmly, he says, "You look awful. We're going to get some sun. You'll feel better once you get outside."

If only her alarm had gone off. If only she'd watched the funeral already. If only she didn't have to fight Ken. "I'm so mixed up. I need to be part of Di's funeral in some way. It feels like we killed a princess—"

Ken uses his dad's psychiatrist tone of voice, the one that says, *I'm right and I have a hundred textbook cases to back me up.* "It's unhealthy to wallow in this all day. Morbid. I thought you wanted to be your own person. Take charge of your life and all that. So let go of Princess Di. She was one big photo op. Royal fluff."

Diana's head feels thicker than a bag of used cotton balls. "No, she was a real person. Funerals are to say good-bye to a person, right? And it's okay to cry—"

Ken puts his hand under her elbow. "Trust me." He leads her toward the door and opens it. "This is too beautiful a day to waste. In two weeks, there'll be movies of Di's funeral. In two weeks, it'll be raining and you can watch it then. You gotta live for today, and today we're meant for the beach."

Ken's arguments are like a spiderweb. She can't find where they start. She resists by silently holding onto the door.

He puts his arm around her, coaxing. "Okay. So bring your Walkman. We won't go to Kits. We'll go to Third Beach at

Stanley Park and nobody you know will see you crying. I can jog on the seawall." He inspects her face. "Did you know your eyes are red? I mean, like, right up to your eyebrows. Not your best, Diana."

Why can't Ken be . . . *nicer?* Maybe Ken needs a few problems.

"Matthew!" she calls into the house. "We're going to the beach. NOW!" Turning to Ken, she explains, "My mom's at work so we have to take him."

Matthew bombs past them, out the front door. "Watch this, sicko."

Ken groans as Matthew catapults through the open car window, disappearing into the leather seats. "Your brother's such a," he catches himself, "a monkey. He belongs in the jungle."

There's a strange clarity to the air; maybe it's the absence of smog. Behind them Grouse Mountain glistens as if someone had dribbled white icing on the peak of a wedding cake. They get in the car and head south. Diana remembers her favorite image of Princess Di—where she seems wide-eyed in the headlights—and shudders. She turns on the radio, finds the funeral coverage. Ken flips to another station. "It's not starting for a few minutes. We need music. Something upbeat."

She's tempted to scream, jump out of the car, and run back home. She takes a deep breath. She can't leave Matthew with Ken. A fight's brewing and she resents it big-time. Why can't she watch the funeral and say good-bye to Princess Di like the rest of the world? Maybe the whole world belongs in therapy.

"Your monkey brother has climbed on the ledge under the

back window. Can't you make him sit like a normal human being?"

"I'm closer to the mountains this way," they hear from the back.

Diana nods approval. If there's one thing she's sure about, it's Matthew. She loves the way Matthew seeks out high places. Whenever he can, he shimmies up telephone poles, doorframes, furniture. Such a harmless way of getting high.

"What's normal?"

For once, Ken doesn't have an answer.

As they cross Lion's Gate Bridge, she turns on her Walkman and secures the earphones. To the west the sun sparkles on the water. Dozens of colorful sailboats catch the morning winds and head out to sea. But Diana's watching another scene, the one the commentators are describing—huge, hushed crowds lining the streets of London to watch the cortege approach Westminster Abbey. With the continuous tolling of the tenor bell, Diana sinks more deeply into a state of mourning, barely aware of reaching Stanley Park, turning right, passing the Kodak moment at the Hollow Tree, parking, walking, finding a perfect spot on the beach for Ken.

Matthew kicks white sand. He hates the beach.

"Too flat," he complains, showering sand for the second time onto Ken's blanket.

Before Ken can smack him, Matthew takes off for the tall lifeguard chair. Diana half-watches Matthew scamper up the red chair and jump on Fred the Lifeguard. Fred's a Chinese guy she recognizes from school. Matthew has told her before that Fred the Lifeguard is a whole lot nicer than Ken the Boyfriend.

Ken pulls her earphones off. "Your brother found perfect company. He sure knows how to pick 'em."

"Fred? What's wrong with him?" She pushes Ken's hand away and replaces the earphones.

Ken laughs. "Remember, that huge thing with the stars he drove to the prom? I saw it in the parking lot. I mean, *hey, babe,* want a ride in my—"

She waves a warning hand, glaring at him. "Shhh," she whispers. "London is mourning. The whole world. It's unbelievably quiet."

Ken opens up the beach bag, pulls out a measuring tape, and measures his muscles, quads, and biceps. He jots down numbers in a little black notebook. Then he shakes the measuring tape in Diana's face, motions her to hold up her arms. Suddenly, she realizes that the size of her waist is directly proportional to the likelihood of Ken ever being nice.

He pulls up one earphone and says in a confidential, sexy voice. "You're getting smaller, and I'm getting bigger."

"Shhhh. They're in the church. Elton John is going to sing a song he wrote for her. Don't you want to listen?"

"You don't know a good thing when you're looking right at him."

He slathers oil on his skin, then straps weights around his wrists. "I'm outta here."

She wishes he'd sit with her. Stop with the body business. Suddenly, she knows what she needs. She's ravenously hungry, for food, for attention, for a friend.

"Please listen, Ken. It's so sad to think she'll never get to hear it. There was an ordinary person inside of her, too."

"Snap out of it. She's dead. God, you look terrible. I'm running sixteen K today. I'll bring you a Diet Coke on my way back. A little caffeine might perk you up." He runs off, kicking back a spiteful shower of sand, forcing her to close her eyes.

She scrunches her knees to her head and starts rocking, humming along to Elton John, thinking of Marilyn Monroe and Princess Di. Why is it important to be pretty when it messes up your life so much?

And then she can't sing anymore, or think. She's bawling her eyes out, a real good cry, the heaving shoulders, let-it-all-out, snot-flowing, mascara-running, heartbreaking kind of cry.

When she stops, the song's been over a while. Her earphones have slipped off. She feels as drained as the old porcelain bathtub at home. A sound enters her conscious space. It's quiet and reassuring. Without looking up, she recognizes the rhythmic shush of the waves. It's the sound of water. The sound fills her being until it is inside her, outside her; there are no more boundaries. She's part of the sea and the white sand beneath her and the salty breeze, of every living thing. . . . Maybe Princess Di is too?

Something warm touches the cool skin of her arm. It's a small hand. She looks up and sees Matthew's freckled face. There's someone beside him. Bigger, older, darker. Fred. In red shorts. White zinc on his nose. Instinctively, she wipes under her eyes, trying to clean up.

Fred kneels down beside Matthew. "Are you okay? You listening to the funeral?"

She nods.

"We saw you from the lifeguard stand. My mom and my sisters have been crying all week. Why didn't you stay home and watch it on TV?"

Of course she should have. She was an idiot not to. Why does she let Ken bully her? She shakes her head, starting to cry again.

Matthew pokes Fred. "You're a lifeguard. You're supposed to make her feel better."

"Right." Fred gives Diana an awkward little hug and pats her shoulders, staring at her like she's a kid who's lost her family at the shopping mall.

Her face rubs accidentally against his shoulder.

"Go ahead. Use my T-shirt. I've got more."

She apologizes. There's a black mascara mess on his red sleeve.

"I meant it. It's okay. Really. My mom uses Tide."

She smiles.

"Say, you look like you lost weight with all that crying. Want a milkshake? Extra-large, chocolate? They're unbelievable. On a terrible day like this we should blow my paycheck at the snack bar."

"She only drinks Diet Coke," says Matthew.

Fred shudders in disgust. "Well, you could slap me silly with a frozen salmon."

Diana can't help it—she laughs. "That's a goofy expression."

"I've got more. My family's big on ancient Chinese sayings."

He's teasing, right? She looks at Matthew. He's grinning. "Told ya."

Fred and Matthew zigzag around big driftwood logs as they head for the steep steps that climb the hill to the snack bar. Matthew jumps up and down beside Fred like he's on some kind of pogo stick with a long-life battery. Then they both start to run up the steps. It's a race.

It's nice to see them having fun ... fun? Oh no, this isn't a day for fun. Diana remembers the funeral and fumbles for the earphones, putting them back on. Princess Di's brother is speaking. He's blaming the paparazzi. They hounded Di. She could never relax and live a normal, ordinary life.

Normal, ordinary life. That's it. What she's been wanting all summer. Ordinary, extraordinary. Like the ocean.

During the hymn and prayers that follow, Diana spins off into a fantasy. It's *her* funeral. . . . She's the Canadian Rose from North Vancouver. The church is strewn with flowers, lined with mourners. Ken jogs up and down the aisles. All the girls watch him and then ... *Oh no!* Ken goes ballistic, yells, "It's your monkey brother!" Matthew swings through the fantasy, up to the front of the church, shimmies up to the top of the pulpit, and flings himself out over the crowds. . . .

Someone sits beside her. Stunned, it takes her a second to return to reality.

She focuses. It's Matthew and Fred. Back. They're drinking milkshakes. Long, slow slurps. The thick chocolate milk, rich with ice cream, flows up the clear straws, disappears into their mouths. She can smell chocolate, almost taste it as she salivates. She removes the earphones, starving.

"Want some?" says Fred.

She shakes her head.

"Scared of backwash?"

She smiles. "You're funny." She looks at him carefully. "Are you ever serious?"

He doesn't answer with another joke, but pushes back the straight, black hair that has spilled over his forehead. He stares at her, equally careful. His eyes are intelligent. Alert.

"Yeah," he says. "I can be serious."

"She's scared of fat," says Matthew.

Maybe it's the funeral, or embarrassment, or the smell of chocolate, but she grabs Fred's milkshake—"I'm not scared of anything!"—slurps what's left of it, tips it way back, slurp, slurp, slurp, every last drop.

"Ah," she sighs, chin up. "I'd forgotten how good they taste."

"You have a nice smile. And all that mascara looks better on my T-shirt."

Matthew scans the beach hopefully. "Where's Ken? Did he drown?"

Diana shakes her head decisively. "Not yet. I think he's heading for the rhubarb."

Fred claps his hands together. "Hey, my family uses that expression too, only no one knows what it means. We thought my great-grandfather messed up translating an old proverb. Honest."

Diana's mind is starting to work. She remembers the vehicle occupying several spaces in the parking lot and Ken's comment. She points in the direction of the parking lot hidden by dense trees.

"Did you drive a Winnebago to the prom? Is the one in the parking lot yours?"

Fred nods. "My parents'. None of my friends could afford a limo for the prom. I surprised them with a real stretch. It's great for work—there's even a shower."

She jumps up. "Oh my God," she says, staring at him aggressively. No more deer eyes. "And a TV?"

Fred looks confused, then nods with understanding. "Oh, right. I get it. You want to watch the funeral. Go ahead. Here's the key. You can cry all you like in privacy. Matthew and I will go save a few people until my shift is over. Then we'll join you. I can give you guys a ride home if you want."

Diana nods. Matthew goes pogo wild, running circles around Fred as they head for the lifeguard chair. Diana starts to pack Ken's things into his beach bag, then drops everything, shaking her head as she scolds herself: "Just dump him! And don't clean up his stuff!"

She picks up the measuring tape, cinches it around the waist of the milkshake container, and shoves it into the sand beside Ken's blanket.

Just as she's about to head for the parking lot, she turns sharply and listens, as if someone had just called her. She stares for a long time at the ocean. Awesome. The shush is still there on the water and here, right here inside her.

A TINY DROP OF OCEAN SPRAY floats into view, glitters briefly in the late summer sun before dissolving into nothing, into the clean, shiny skin of her cheek.

The Piano Lesson

SHE CLIMBS THE STAIRS to the third floor of the conservatory. David, her piano teacher, is waiting. He teaches in a large studio with his tabby cat, Tripod, and always wears a T-shirt covered in cat hair, along with black jeans and turquoise running shoes. Every few months, however, he colors the halo of his hair. Lately, it's been turquoise to match his shoes.

She missed last week's lesson, and he asks if she is okay. She lies and is uneasy because of it. He asks for a C-major scale, the easiest scale on the piano, one she has known since she was six, but he asks for four octaves, top to bottom—he's so contrary!—left hand only. She has never played a scale this way before. It throws her.

"That was fine," he comments. "Good finger action. Too bad it was three octaves. Try the right hand, same thing."

She starts and he interrupts immediately. "No. I want top to bottom."

"I don't play it that way. I always start at the bottom."

"I know. That's the point."

She swears inwardly. But she is well brought up and says

nothing. At least, she used to be. She's feeling brought down since last week.

"Hmm. That was five octaves this time, but I guess that's eight all together. Practice that for me this week, will you? Just the C-major scale. Separate hands. Top to bottom."

The other technical exercises are equally disastrous. He opens up the Chopin nocturne. She loves this piece, wants to play it well. "You've memorized it?" he asks.

"I'm trying. I'm having a little trouble."

"What key is it in?"

David *would* ask this question. He takes his role seriously. He is the master, she the student. He won't let her relax, drift into la-la land, and demands that she think about the music she is playing, understand its structure. In the year she has studied with him, her playing has improved dramatically. Last spring she received the second-highest mark in the provincial exams, and her father, who has paid for another year's tuition, is pleased.

But she hasn't practiced for two weeks. Only this morning did she look at the key signature, knowing David would ask his nasty questions at the lesson.

The piece has four sharps in the key signature and is somewhat haunting, in a minor key. She is confident of her answer. "C-sharp minor."

"What's your base note?"

Mouth open, she looks up at the music for help. Too late. He moves in, closes the score, takes it.

"You're in C-sharp minor. What's your base note?"

"C-sharp," she says, staring at a black key on the keyboard. But she's guessing.

"Yes. That's your anchor. Tonic chord, first position." He

stands up and moves the chair well behind her, giving them some psychological, as well as physical distance. He sniffs constantly. He has told her, in confidence, that he has AIDS, and she wonders if the excess of fluid in his nose is a symptom. Bodily fluids have a way of being treacherous.

"Now play the first two lines, please. Remember with Chopin, keep a *cantabile* melody in the right hand, soft accompaniment in the left."

She tries to clear her mind. Focus. All fall she's had trouble memorizing this piece.

Treble trouble. Bass trouble. Boy trouble.

Somehow, the first two lines are in her fingers. She stops thinking, no longer using her brain, and plays from a different part of her inner being. It's like sex with the boy. Turning off the brain and responding with the body. She thinks of the boy. She loves his dark curls and the way he sits, yoga style, when they talk. They are both eighteen, both in first-year university, although he lives in South Carolina, where people linger over syllables and say they go to "ca-a-a-w-w-w-llege"?

"Stop." David moves and stands beside her again. "I can certainly hear the right hand. Only, I wouldn't call it singing." He has a sarcastic tone and a mischievous smile on his face. "That was rather butch for my taste."

She laughs. David shocks her sometimes by giving unusual sexual meanings to music. It makes her think differently. He is outrageous. It's a secret between them. Her father pays for the lessons and assumes that David is a proper Conservatory of Music teacher like the ones who taught her father two generations earlier. She is the daughter of her father's old age, born when he was over fifty. But she is not keeping him young. In fact, last week he looked quite old and unwanted, like an aborted grandfather.

No. Her father would definitely be uncomfortable if he overheard David say her playing was butch or, worse, telling her anecdotes about his dates with truck drivers, engineers, waiters—men from all walks of life and of all nationalities.

David moves back a few steps, megaphones his hand in front of his mouth. "Music is language. It's communicating. It's the voice of God, of your soul and emotions. Do you really think Chopin meant to say, 'Hey, honey, get over here and take your clothes off'?"

She giggles. So does he. Already she feels the depression that has overwhelmed her during the last few weeks lift, like a few wrong notes, Latin calypso in the middle of a requiem.

"What does *nocturne* mean?"

She took Latin for two years in high school. "Something to do with nighttime." She smiles, suddenly anticipating where David will go with this.

"Good answer. Especially, I would think, to do with *bedtime* activities. So I want this to be delicate. Sensual. As if one fingertip is ever so lightly—" He stops abruptly.

Is there a look on her face? A memory of the boy, last summer, left on her cheekbones?

"Start from the top of page two."

Oh God. Her mind goes completely blank. So do her fingers. She places them on the piano, right thumb on E, but . . . what goes with it? What is the chord in the left hand? Her body is letting her down. The memory is not there.

"What key are you in?" David repeats.

"G-sharp major," she says, desperately remembering the lesson from two weeks ago. She knows that G-sharp is the fifth note of the C-sharp minor scale. It has a perfect relationship to C-sharp minor.

"No."

"Okay," she fumbles. "How about G-sharp minor? F-sharp minor? I don't know, David—"

"It's A-major." David cuts her off swiftly. He loves accuracy. He may fool around with lovers, but never, *never* with music.

Tripod, David's beloved cat, jumps onto the windowsill. He is three-legged and barely makes it, but he manages, then lies on the wide sill purring. If she plays well, Tripod will jump down and approach her, wrap himself around her calves, rubbing with pleasure. But Tripod is looking lazily out the window, uninterested in her. She takes this as a bad sign.

"A-major?" She is incredulous. What is Chopin doing in A-major? How did this transition happen?

David goes into a mini-lecture on harmony, the relationship of A-major to C-sharp minor. He finds a pencil and prods her, harasses her into analyzing all the changes of key on the second page. There are too many. Her mind is spinning.

He flips up the music holder on the piano and returns the marked-up page so she can read it. She does not want to analyze. She resents thinking; she wants to let herself go. Somewhere in her mind, she knows she should be examining her life like a piece of music. What if she tells David, her brilliant teacher, her dilemma? Would he force her to examine the fingering and harmony, the rhythm and behavior of the boy and herself, so that she understands their relationship? Would she know what to do then? Not just with her spirit and her body, but with her brain, so that she could translate their love from top to bottom, in any direction, and know how to play this out?

But that is not why she comes to the studio, is it? She chastises herself: David is just her piano teacher.

She is lonely. She misses the boy. Her mind spins again.

"Divide the page into sections," David lectures. "Play the sections randomly until you know them so intimately, they're in your deep tissue. You can't memorize a piece unless you understand it. Play the third bar in the first line, please."

Deep tissue. She plays the third bar thinking about the size of an unwanted ten-week old fetus, smaller than her thumb.

"And again."

She plays the bar again, noticing it is in F-sharp minor.

"Good. That was better. Now turn to page three. Let me hear the first bar in the fourth line."

She looks at the third page, takes a deep breath and plays the requested bar. In the first two beats of the first bar in the fourth line, there are thirty-five notes in the right hand against four eighth notes in the left. She has practiced this many times, so many times, she can now, amazingly, do it, though she doesn't know how. It seems a bit like happiness: some days it just *happens.*

"That was beautiful." David sits beside her and takes her hand, massages it gently. "Relax your hands. Let your wrists be still. Articulate your fingers. You're supported in the back"—he places a hand lightly against the small of her back—"in your shoulders, right down to your fingers. You don't throw weight from your shoulders to produce sound, you don't need excessive movement. Good sound comes from a well-articulated finger."

She likes the feel of David's hand against the small of her

back. It calms her; something happens inside her when his hand is there. She feels stronger, as if she has a center that is connected with the universe, as if she could be anything she wanted to be, do anything she wanted to do, without so many consequences.

Last week in the day unit, a nurse had started asking her questions. Too many questions. She'd sat between her father and the boy, spinning out of control, unable to talk. Her father had answered for her. Finally, the nurse had gone away. She'd held the boy's hand—after all, he'd come up from South Carolina to be with her for this event—but it was her father's hand she longed to hold. She shared with him the same strong shape of hand and long, fine fingers. Made to play the piano. But she could not remember holding her father's hand, *ever.* It was hardly the moment to begin.

"Shall I play it for you?" David asks.

They change places. David's eyes are very bad. He gets them checked at the hospital frequently. He adjusts his thick, heavily framed, green glasses to read the music. She remembers the odd message he recorded on his answering machine—"Greetings, carbon-based bipeds!"—and as he starts to play, she thinks that he is part angel. Then all language and thought leave her and she is in the music, the way she likes best, as close to God as she will ever be.

When the piece is over, she knows what nocturnal activities the music is describing. David is wrong. It is *not* about sex. It is a lullaby, a window opening to heaven, a place she likes, a place she knows is the beginning and the end, even for unwanted carbon-based bipeds that are no bigger than her thumb.

There is a long silence. Tripod has jumped off the windowsill and is purring, rubbing himself against David's legs. She would do the same if she were a cat, but she can't purr nor think of adequate words. So she smiles at her teacher. It's enough.

David smiles back, passes her the music and reads her thoughts. "That's what I'm here for—to inspire you."

"Thank-you," she tells him. The lesson is over. It is time to go. She has made up her mind. She has to tell him.

"I have to cancel my lessons. I'm leaving. I won't be here next week . . . or for a while. I'm quitting school, everything. I'm going to South Carolina." She feels she owes him more of an explanation. She fights her shyness to tell him. "I have to find out what key I'm in."

She can't look at him. She senses unasked questions, but he pauses, maybe kindly, and says, "The nocturne—do you know what key it ends in?"

She shakes her head.

"You'll figure it out. Call me when you're ready to study again. I'll be leaving the conservatory at Christmas. Teaching privately. You've got my number."

She leaves the large, rambling redbrick building. Windows are open on the upper floors, where the rooms get hot and stuffy. She hears bars of music floating out to her like random thoughts, bits of jumbled conversations. She wonders how far they could carry on a good breeze, if she would be able to hear them all the way from South Carolina. It is such a long way from here, a different country really.

She lifts her head at the sound of a familiar melody. Hey! The last bars of the nocturne. Is it possible? The music is no longer in a sad, minor key; it sounds sweet, like happiness. And, suddenly, she knows what key the piece ends in. She opens the manuscript to double-check and smiles. She's right. The C-sharp minor nocturne ends, amazingly, in C-sharp major.

Chopin just blows her away.

Skating Home

"So. Do they fit?" Lisa asked.

I was putting on Lisa's old skates. She'd dragged me with her to Icing on the Cake, Edmonton's newest downtown rink. Friday nights, she'd promised, the Cake was really hot.

"They're okay," I answered. "A bit tight. Course, I don't feel anything with my no-toes." That's what we called them. After the accident, other kids had nicknamed me Toeless Tess. But Lisa was my best friend. She'd gone skating with me that day, four years ago. Between us, we just called them no-toes.

I looked up. *"Ahhh . . . the most beautiful man skated by."*

Lisa stuck her face beside mine, looked in the same direction. "Who? What? Where?"

I pointed after a dark-haired stranger in a tight, white turtleneck. His swelling shoulders flickered through the crowd like a strobe light. "He looks like Stojko, only better."

"That guy? Forget it. He never asks anyone to skate." Abruptly, Lisa yanked me to my feet. "Careful. Drooling is *not* sexy."

I followed her, stepping carefully over the wide threshold of the rink. Ever since the accident on the river, I'd had to watch my balance. Skating was risky business.

Other kids from my high school glided past. I hadn't been on skates since grade eight. I forced myself into the surging crowd.

"How'd I let you talk me into this?" I moaned.

A pulse of male energy streaked by. *Him!* I caught a trace of his sweat. "Just smell that. Eau de Stojko," I sighed.

"You're in heat, Tess," Lisa laughed beside me. "He figure skates. I think he plays for the other team."

"Lisa!"

She rolled her eyes in self-defense. "What? He was with another guy the first few times he came here."

"So? How about us? We used to figure skate, and we came together too."

Lisa puckered her purple-glossed lips as if waiting for a kiss. I swatted her. "What do you know about him?"

"Only that he works at the MicroPlay on Jasper. He looks . . . old."

"Wow, look at that! A perfect toe-loop!"

In the far corner, Stojko turned gracefully, then began to pick up speed, like a hawk in a forest seeking prey. *Oh, let it be me,* I prayed.

I skated backward to watch him, my feet with a memory of their own, remembering how to cross over. As he approached, I sent him my most brilliant smile.

He caught it . . . and knocked me over. I spun on my back, helpless as an overturned turtle. When I stopped, he was standing over me.

"Sorry," he said. "I shouldn't be skating so fast in this crowd."

"No," I said, sitting up. "It's my fault." I took off my headband so I could toss my best feature, my long waves of wheat-colored hair.

Behind Stojko, Lisa stuck her finger in her mouth. Her face said, *gag me.*

Stop with the hair, I told myself. *Say something fascinating.*

"I used to figure skate. Before I had an accident four years ago."

He smiled sympathetically. Maybe he liked a girl in distress?

"You skate . . . like Stojko," I stuttered.

He leaned forward slightly, as if pleased. *No* . . . he was offering me his hand.

"Thanks. I used to dream of being as good as Elvis. Now I just hope I get accepted into law school."

Lisa interrupted before she moved away. "I'm going to get a hot chocolate. All that skating. I'm so thirsty I could throw up."

I ignored her, calculating. He looked about five years older than me. Maybe early twenties? "U of A?" I asked. Cool. Incredibly mature.

"No. Toronto. Maybe McGill. I want to head back east." He slipped his hand under my elbow as if it were the most natural thing in the world.

There was an immediate meltdown inside me, inside maybe all of Alberta. I felt myself being carried away somewhere on a strange, new current. *East!* I prayed. *Let me head east!*

His name was Guy Daniels and we skated all evening, talked about families, friends, and figure skating.

The Cake closed at midnight. Guy had a car and he offered us a ride home. Lisa kept her thoughts to herself until we got out at my place. I stared dreamily after Guy's disappearing brake-lights. She started in on me like a Greek chorus from one of those tragedies we'd studied at school.

"You don't know that guy. I don't have a good feeling about him."

"How'd you know his name?" I laughed. "Only, you pronounce it *gee* with a hard *g;* rhymes with *me.*"

"Wake up, Tess. Who cares how you say his name? You don't know anything about him."

I started singing our favorite song. "'I won't ask who you are, who you loved . . .'"

Eyes doomy-gloomy, Lisa didn't join in. Under the street-light, she was one long shadow stretching down the street.

I kept singing, "'. . . baby, just love me.'"

Abruptly, she turned away, her shadow like a swinging door, getting smaller, disappearing under the light, then getting larger again, until she was part of the night.

HE PROMISED TO PHONE, and he did. I liked that about him, but I was a prairie girl at the ocean for the first time: I liked everything about him. We saw a movie together, *Sliding Doors,* where a woman's life took two possible paths from a single moment. Either way, the ending—her fate—was the same.

After the movie, we stopped at a Second Cup coffee shop and sat on the stools at the window. "Did you ever have a moment like that, when your life took a wrong turn?" Guy asked, stirring his hot cranberry drink with a cinnamon stick.

I watched, hypnotized by the whirlpool in the red liquid, suddenly remembering red skin, freezing tissue.

"Yeah," I confessed. "Christmas, grade eight. I was starting to skate in competitions, and I asked for really good figure skates: high-end Risports. They cost way more than my parents could afford."

I paused. This felt dangerous, telling Guy my secret. What if he recoiled like the other boys?

Guy kept stirring his drink.

I'd look stupid if I stopped, so I continued. "During the holidays, Lisa and I decided to skate on the creek behind my place. For once, it had frozen smooth. We skated down to the North Saskatchewan. Often there's open water on the river even at forty below, because of the power plant. I had promised my parents I'd take my old skates. The new ones were supposed to be only for competitions, but they were so beautiful, soft and white . . . like angels' wings on my feet."

I paused, lost in the memory. The whirlpool of red liquid was slowing down.

"That was my sliding door moment: putting on my new skates, knowing I should go back and get my old ones."

"What happened?" he asked softly.

"I hit a thin spot and fell through." I stared into Guy's dark eyes, but saw instead river water pooling around my feet.

I struggled to continue. "Luckily, we were near shore, and I made it to the bank easily. I remember standing there, staring at my beautiful skates, wet and mucky. My feet were freezing, as cold as that water in the North Saskatchewan, but the worst thing was how mad I was at myself. God, I felt stupid. Every second was agony walking back to where we'd left our boots. Somehow Lisa got me home, and we snuck into my place. Before she left, Lisa begged me to tell my parents. But I ignored her. It took a long time before I stopped shaking. My feet . . . they felt pretty strange but not too bad. Lisa must have told her parents because they phoned mine. My mom and dad came in my room, all white-faced and serious. You know what I said?"

Guy shook his head.

"I said I didn't deserve those skates . . . but my dad said, 'Forget the skates. Show us your feet.'"

"Your parents sound okay," Guy said, and I nodded.

I shivered, hating to tell the end of the story. "But see, I'd forgotten about frostbite, how you lose feeling with it. It's like an anesthetic, total freezing till you wake up. In a weird way, your body betrays you. I showed my parents my feet. My toes were bright red and two were starting to blister. Dad carried me out to the car and drove like a maniac to the hospital."

I couldn't look at Guy anymore or the red drink on the table between us. I stared at the half-eaten blueberry muffin on my plate. "The doctors were afraid of gangrene. They cut off the two toes that were blistered. I can't think of anything good that's come of it, except that last Friday was the first time I've skated in four years"—I decided to take a risk—"and I met you."

During my confession my hair had slipped down over my face. Now through its curtain, I heard laughter and footsteps as people left the coffee shop. Cold air swirled around my exposed ankles. Then I felt Guy's fingers gently push my hair back and linger on my cheek.

I looked at him. His dark eyes were studying my lips. Ever so slowly he brought his face close and kissed me. His lips were even warmer than his hands and a switch turned on in my body.

When he pulled away, I leaned after him, hungry for more.

"What about you, Guy? Did *you* ever have a sliding door moment?"

He nodded. But a look came over his face, more like a closed door. "I came to Edmonton with"—he glanced awkwardly around the coffee shop—"someone. But it hasn't worked out. We split up. And last Friday . . . I met you."

It was the perfect moment to ask more, but I didn't want to know about someone else—only that whoever she was had gone.

The next Friday night we met at the Cake. This time, when I stepped onto the ice, Guy put his arm around my waist, pulling me close. A hot current zapped through me where our bodies touched: my shoulder melted into his chest, my hip flirted with his thigh.

Zap. I was on. The music pulsed between us. I turned my brain off and just skated, his partner, our legs thrusting, gliding together.

We were electric.

I saw Lisa and *zapped* her a smile.

She didn't smile back. "What do you know about him?" she hissed in my ear.

"He's not gay. Go away!"

He asked if I wanted to go back to his place. I did.

He put on some soft music and pulled me over to the sofa. I told him my feet were cold and he asked if he could take off my socks. He held my bare feet in his warm hands, but I shivered with embarrassment as he looked at the scar that replaced my toes.

"I think you're beautiful," he said.

I began to relax, enjoying the heated pressure of his fingers on my skin. I watched his eyes as he spoke, all the while letting his hands move slowly up from my feet.

"We don't really need toes," he said. "They're useless. You're centuries ahead."

I was dying to kiss him, to feel the weight of his body, the lightness of his lips. "I was so afraid to show you, but now . . ."

"Now?"

And, finally, he was kissing me, moving his hands, pulling off his shirt, then mine, cool air on our hot skin. I closed my eyes. I was skating again in my beautiful skates. The ice was smooth and strong, and this time I knew it would be different. This time I'd skate all the way home.

ON THE SAME DAY my period didn't show, Guy didn't show either.

It was early spring, May. My period came every twenty-eight days, as regular as Mom making coffee in the morning and Dad giving me a ride to school.

For six weeks, Guy and I had had this routine. He'd wait for me after school before his evening shift started at MicroPlay. But that day, I waited two hours for him before going home. I called his apartment, listened to the *ring, ring, ring.* Then I called MicroPlay. The answering machine came on, which meant they were busy. Maybe . . . they must have asked him to come in early.

The next day after school, still no period, still no Guy. I was beginning to feel prickles of fear. I told myself he'd show. *Something* had to show.

I sat on a rocky retaining wall at the front of the school watching the parking lot empty. The wall's sharp ledge cut through my skirt and into my thighs, but I had lost sensation in every part of my body.

Guy, where are you? I have to tell you something.

I didn't see Lisa until she was right in front of me. We'd barely spoken for the six weeks I'd been seeing Guy. I knew she disapproved. I'd lied to my parents, said I was at her place whenever I'd been with Guy. Only, this time she never told. She never said a word.

"He's gone," she said, her voice I-told-you-so.

I frowned. Her arms were folded across her chest and even her spiky, bleached hair seemed mad at me.

"I had to take my brother to MicroPlay last night," she continued. "I didn't see Guy. He works evenings, right? Every evening except Friday? I asked where he was. The owner said he quit two days ago. He got accepted into some university down east."

Her words were sharp things, jabbing at me.

"He wouldn't do that."

She grabbed my arms. "He's gone, Tess."

The rocky wall cracked beneath me. I'd hit a treacherous spot. Dark water was rising around my ankles. Any second now river water would seep out of my mouth, my eyes.

"Lisa," I said, too scared for secrets, "my period's late."

She groaned and gave my arms a hard tug. "Oh, Tess."

"All that sex education from Mrs. Palmerston . . . wasted on me. I don't know why, but I didn't use anything. . . ."

She squeezed both my wrists. "You didn't use a condom?"

"For God's sake, Lisa!" How dare she? "You think I carry them in my pocket? Like with my lunch money? Where do you keep yours? In your purse?"

"Jeez, Tess. They're easy to get. They're in the washroom at school."

"We never did it in the washroom at school."

"Oh, you idiot! You could've put one in your pocket."

I yanked my wrists free, wanting to slap her. "Okay, Little Miss Pharmacy!" I yelled. "These things should happen to you. *You* would be prepared!"

Her cheeks flushed red. Immediately, I regretted saying it. What was I doing? I was yelling at my best friend. "Oh, Lisa. What'll I do?" I wailed.

Her eyes stopped blazing then. My old friend's eyes were back, clear and blue, hurting for me. She wrapped her arms around me.

"No toes. No brains," she whispered in my ear. "You gotta get tested, remember? I'll come with you, if you want."

"Oh God," I moaned. "A pregnancy test."

"If I were you, I'd be more worried about the other one."

The little hairs on the back of my neck stood up. Oh no. I hadn't even considered *that*.

Every September, Mrs. Palmerston chalked an address and phone number into the upper right-hand corner of the blackboard. It stayed there all year: *Hassle Free Clinic*. You could get an anonymous HIV test there. In the safety of the back of the classroom, we'd joked about the code names we'd give, like Marilyn Monroe or Madonna or—Lisa's favorite— Mother Teresa.

I wished myself back in time, back in that classroom, making jokes, but my feet were stuck in a block of ice. There was no going back, no going forward either.

Lisa must've chipped out my feet and carried me to the clinic; I don't know how else I could have gotten there. It was like the time at the river, only, this time every cell in my body had crystallized with fear.

Slowly, I realized I was in a snowy white room with Lisa beside me. A receptionist was staring at me, her lips moving.

The frames of her glasses were deep green, the same weird color as her eyes. Her lips moved again. "A name," they said. "I need a name."

From the back corner of my mind, I answered, "Teresa."

Lisa groaned. The receptionist wrote it down.

"I'll give you a number, your identifying number at the clinic. Okay?"

I nodded.

"Three-oh-five. I need a phone number."

Without thinking, I gave my home number.

"Go down the hall to the first room on your right. There's a counselor there. She'll explain the tests. Tell her your number."

I nodded and repeated obediently, "Three-oh-five." Then I turned to Lisa. "I have to do this on my own."

Lisa nodded. "Okay," she said. "I'll wait here."

Down the hall, first room on the right, I became number 305. The counselor told me about the pregnancy test and then about the ELISA test, the screening of blood for HIV antibodies. If I had antibodies, the test would be nonreactive. But if the test results were positive, it still might mean something else: I might be lucky and have herpes or a sleep disorder. Something I could live with.

"We'll phone you when the lab results are in," the counselor said. "But we won't give results over the phone. You'll have to come in person. It's critical that you come in quickly. If you're positive, treatment should be started immediately."

My heart pounded. HIV positive? Treatment? *Guy, where are you?* I wondered, wishing he were here to take care of things. *Stupid thought.* I switched off my brain and rolled up my sleeve, waiting for the nurse.

I was so scared, a small miracle took place, a thaw in my

deep tissues. Blood began to flow right then and there as the nurse tied a length of rubber around my arm "to get a good vein."

"You better hurry," I said. Blood was leaking from me, sticky and wet between my legs. I wasn't pregnant. But I wasn't Tess anymore either, not even a no-toe, no-brain Tess. I was no-name number 305.

I rolled down my sleeve and went home to wait for a hassle-free call.

DAY AFTER DAY, I waited, hoping for a different miracle. My wishful-thinking brain cells were still kicking: *He'll come back. Guy loves me.* As casually as I could manage, I visited the superintendent of Guy's apartment, then MicroPlay. *Did they know where he'd gone?* Back east. *Had he said anything?* He was happy he'd been accepted into law school.

At first, I made up excuses for him. He must have been afraid I wouldn't want him to go. Day after day, I was sure the phone would ring, but whenever it did, it was Lisa, checking to see how I was.

Every day I allowed myself to sit on the retaining wall, indulging my childish hopes. But every day he wasn't there. The tulip leaves were, each day a little higher. They were pushing up green letters from the dark earth, spelling out two easy-reader words: Go Home.

TWO WEEKS LATER, walking home, I noticed Mom on the front step, waiting for me like she used to when I was little, holding out my Winnie-the-Pooh mug.

"How's my princess? Tea?" She smiled. "Three spoonfuls of honey."

"Hey, Mom. Thanks."

I took the cup. Steam rose and disappeared above us, into the blue sky.

"Why so down?"

"I don't know. Maybe it's the French test tomorrow. It's on tricky verbs, like *espérer*, 'to wish,' where the accent changes."

"Bun chance, cherry," Mom said, giving her fossilized version of *bonne chance, chérie*, all that remained from her five years of high-school French. "Good luck, dear." Those three nonsense words usually made me smile. Not today.

"Speaking of wishes," Mom continued, "you'll be seventeen in a few weeks. Got a wish close to your heart?"

I was holding back tears, longing to tell her about the clinic test.

"Funny thing," she said, sipping her tea. "There've been several calls lately . . ."

My wishful thinking starting kicking wildly.

". . . for a Teresa," Mom finished slowly. "Some lady keeps saying, 'If you know a Teresa please get her to call me.'"

Thank god I was holding a hot drink. It kept the freezing at bay. Without it, my hand might have fallen off, just cracked off into Mom's lap. *Guess what, Mom. I may lose more of me.*

Should I tell her now? Panicking, I sipped my tea. It burned going down. "Teresa," I started. But I couldn't. Just one more lie. "She's the new girl at school. Doesn't speak much English. I gave her my number."

The phone rang inside the kitchen. Startled, I spilled brown drops on the step. A few splashed onto my mother's canvas runners.

Mom checked her watch. "I told the woman I'd ask my daughter. She said she'd call back after four. Maybe that's her." She reached for my cup. "I'll hold that, sweetie. You go answer it. It's probably for that Teresa girl."

It was. It was the clinic. Number 305's results were in.

I NEVER WENT to the clinic to get the results. I told Lisa I did, that I was fine; I'd learned a terrible lesson. Lisa decided we should celebrate by going to the Cake Friday nights. It stayed open until the end of June, long after the tulips had blossomed and died.

I skated circles around the cloudy ice, preferring when someone asked Lisa to skate and I was left alone. Guy hadn't left a forwarding address. He hadn't called or written. I'd stopped making excuses for him. When the song came on that I associated with him, I clung to the sideboards, my hands against my ears, muffling those words: *Please won't you love me.*

My mind was numb from replaying every conversation, every moment we'd spent together. How could he leave like that—without a word? Was he sick? Was I?

On the Friday the Cake closed, that damn song came on again. God, how I hated it! I felt so red-hot sick of lies, I wanted to melt the ice. I began to skate.

I imagined the clinic. The receptionist with those green glasses growing out of her eyes. The hallway. The door on the right. There was something I wanted her to know. What was it?

I skated faster, imagining the counselor's office, playing out our conversation. How would it start? Then it came to me. I'd start from the beginning. I'd tell her, "My name is Tess."

About the Author

Anne Laurel Carter is the author of from *Poppa* and *Tall in the Saddle,* an American Booksellers Association Pick of the Lists picture book. Her previous novels include *In the Clear, The Girl on Evangeline Beach* and *Our Canadian Girl Elizabeth: Bless This House.*

"Leaving the Iron Lung," included in this collection, received the 1999 Vicky Metcalf Short Story Award. "The Piano Lesson," also included in this collection, won the Thistledown Young Adult Short Story Contest.